The SHUTOUT *Girl*

by Glenn Parker

Produced by:

FriesenPress

Suite 300 – 852 Fort Street
Victoria, BC, Canada V8W 1H8

www.friesenpress.com

Distributed to the trade by The Ingram Book Company

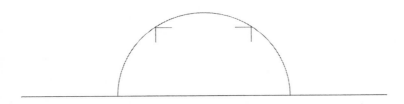

DEDICATION

To Manon Rheume Who Blazed A Trail For Young Women Who Want To Become Not Only Outstanding Goaltenders, But Goaltenders Who Can Compete Against Men.

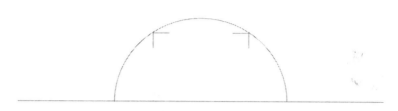

A NOTE TO ASPIRING FEMALE ATHLETES:

Girls competing against guys has become a topic of interest in the last few years. In some sports such as football and even hockey, this is a very difficult feat for most girls, if not all of them. In other sports such as golf, competition between the sexes is not quite as difficult, although the balance still tips vastly toward the male.

Whenever a female competes against males and is successful, it usually makes headlines and is a feat to be celebrated. In hockey about the only position that a girl could compete with a guy is as a goaltender. In this story, Katherine does this and does it with grace and style.

I always look forward to competitions in which girls compete and win against their much larger and stronger opponents. I hope you enjoy what Katherine achieved and find inspiration in it.

G.P.

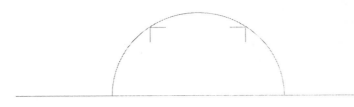

CHAPTER 1

(The Winter of 1980)

My name is Katherine Rollins, but some people call me Kat for short. I prefer Katherine but either name is okay with me. I'm the only girl in our family. I have four older brothers. Sometimes it's a blessing, but at other times it can be pretty trying. What I mean by that is they don't often respect the fact that I'm a girl, that I'm different from them and that I'm not impressed by their rough – housing and silly antics.

Even though I'm only fourteen and have my own room and like my privacy, they don't seem to respect that either. They come into my room anytime they want just as though it was their room. I've complained to my parents but they just smile and shrug their shoulders. "Tell them to get lost," my dad says, but a lot of good that would do.

When I had a lock installed, they all thought that was pretty funny. They just kept knocking on my door, almost driving me crazy. What is it about brothers that makes them such pests?

On the flip side, sometimes they can be very sweet and helpful. They help with my homework sometimes, drive me places and make sure nobody is bothering me. That's kind of nice. Makes me feel safe and all.

We live out in the country about five miles from town beside a small lake. In the winter if we get an early freeze and before it snows too much, we can skate for miles along the edge of the lake. It's a blast.

We live in a large house with four bedrooms. I've got my own room but my brothers have to share one. My oldest brother has a car and we often all climb into it and go into town to shop or go to a movie or just hang out. My parents both work in town so they both have cars as well. Sometimes they give me a lift but most often it's my brother Jed. My mom works part time at our school and teaches piano lessons. My dad works at the local mill. He's the foreman there and works pretty hard according to Mom.

We had chickens for a while, but that didn't turn out too well. We've got a dog named Puck. He's a black Labrador and does his best to drive us all crazy. Of course, we all love him but he does some pretty weird things. For instance, when we play hockey, he wants to play too and keeping him off the rink is a job in itself. Sometimes we have to resort to tying him up in the yard so that he doesn't ruin our game.

We've had a skating rink in the winter ever since I can remember. All four of my brothers play hockey in town at the local arena, but we all skate on our little rink in the back yard. My dad does most of the work, flooding it, keeping it clear of snow and making sure the boards around it are kept in good repair. He also installed floodlights for when it's dark early in the morning. The ice surface is not as big as the arena in town, but it's big enough to play hockey on, something my brothers do all the time. They get up early and skate and play hockey for an hour before going off to school. I do a lot of skating myself and I'm a pretty good skater. My brothers are all really good hockey players and are always talking about playing in the N.H.L. I don't know if they're that good, but they all do well in the local minor hockey leagues.

Jed, the oldest, is 17 and plays Juvenile and is the leading scorer on his team. Michael is sixteen and plays Midget. He's pretty good too. John and Malcolm are 15 and twins and are in their first year of Midget. They aren't identical twins though. John was born 15 minutes before Malcolm so considers himself Malcolm's older brother. He's sturdier than Malcolm and a lot more outgoing. Unfortunately, they have similar temperaments and love to tease me.

My dad played a lot of hockey and was the leading scorer almost every year he played for the local senior team. He had a tryout for one of the N.H.L. teams but from what I can gather, he got so homesick after being away for several weeks, that he just came back home. He missed the farm and his girlfriend (now my mother) and felt like a fish out of water in Toronto. I guess he's just a hometown guy who likes the country life and that's all he really wanted. He's very loyal to my mom and us kids. He'd do anything for us. It's kind of nice having a dad like that.

Anyway, my brothers are always competing against each other on our home rink. Who can skate the fastest, shoot the hardest, body check the hardest. It's an ongoing thing in our family. We are all very competitive. Except me, of course. I couldn't care less. I just enjoy skating a lot because I like to excel at everything I try. I'm good at most things, like school and cooking and I'm a pretty good piano player. I'm not ready for Carnegie Hall or anything like that, but I'm pretty good. At least Mom thinks so. She's my teacher and a very good pianist herself.

I get good grades at school too, mostly A's but sometimes I slip and get a B in Math. My brothers are all good students too but not as good as I am. They're mostly B's and the occasional A in shop and P.E. When they get teasing me about my inability to fix things, my lack of strength or my speed on the ice compared to theirs, I just remind them that I'm an A student and they aren't. It gets them every time. Of course, they know better than to criticize my cooking and baking. They would starve otherwise. They've all got appetites that would probably keep my parents in poverty if they didn't both work.

One of the ongoing problems my brothers have is that they don't have a goalie. They've tried to get me in there a few times but I'm not that stupid. As an alternative, they put a board up against the net, but it's no substitute for a goalie. Once in a while my Dad will go in goal, but he's a forward himself and doesn't like playing goal either. Besides, we don't have any goalie equipment and anybody who plays goalie usually ends up getting a few pucks in places where it really hurts. They've thought about buying goalie equipment, but it's so expensive, none of my brothers wants to put out the money for it.

One day when my brothers were having a particularly competitive game, they began arguing about whether a shot one of the twins made had actually gone into the net. I guess it went in and out so fast, nobody really knew for sure whether it was a goal or not. At the time I was skating in my little part of the rink. Whenever I want to skate when my brothers are playing hockey, they shorten the rink by putting one of the nets part way up the ice. I have to be very careful though, and watch out for flying pucks.

The next thing I know, Jed is skating over toward me with that look on his face that I know only too well. I'm shaking my head even before he gets to me, but that doesn't deter him one bit.

"Come on Katherine, put on some shin pads and play goal for us. I promise, we won't shoot hard ones and we won't raise the puck. Honest." He stood there like I was some kind of dope who would actually believe what he was saying. I've seen my brothers in action and when they get into the heat of battle, they get really carried away. I don't want anything to do with it.

"Not on your life," I said. "I'm not making myself a target for you guys. Do you think I'm crazy?"

Jed looked back at his brothers and shrugged. "Guess we'll have to cancel that little shopping spree we had planned for you," he said. "We were all going to chip in and let you go crazy at the mall. Buy anything you wanted. Within reason of course."

"Really?" I said. I was a real sucker for bribes, especially if it involved buying clothes. My mom always said I had an unusual talent for shopping. I was never sure whether she was serious or just kidding me.

"Really," Jed said. "Right, guys?" My brothers looked a little astonished. "So what do you think?"

"Just when is this shopping spree supposed to take place?" I asked. "And how much can I spend?"

The rest of my brothers had skated over and were standing beside Jed. They were looking at him as though he had lost his mind. "Any time you want," Jed said, ignoring his brothers. "We'll drive you in and you can fill your boots, shop till you drop."

"How much?" I persisted. "After all, making myself a target for you guys to shoot at is worth a lot of dough."

"Yeah, well, a couple of dresses, a pair of shoes maybe. That shouldn't cost too much. What do you think guys?"

"I think you're nuts," Michael offered.

The twins looked at each other. I could almost read their minds. Neither one of them had anything on Scrooge. They had the first nickel they had ever made. "What kind of money are we talking about?" Michael wanted to know.

"How about fifty dollars," Jed suggested. "I'll kick in half of it."

"She has to play goalie anytime we want her, for that much," Malcolm said. "This isn't a one time deal."

"You want me to place my life on the line for a measly fifty dollars? I always thought you guys were a bit thick. Now I know you are if you think I'd fall for a deal like that."

"Okay," Jed said. "How much do you want? We only got so much we can spend."

I stood there making some calculations in my head. I had to figure how much I could get out of them without it being outrageous, an amount that was reasonable and yet would justify my being a goalie for a bunch of rowdies and putting my head on the line. Jed had a part-time job washing cars and pumping gas at the local Chevy dealer and could afford more than the rest.

"At least two hundred. You can afford a hundred, Jed, and the rest of you guys can come up with thirty five dollars each. For that you got me for the season, anytime you want."

I think the amount sort of set them back on their heels. They hadn't expected it, but playing with a goalie even if she was a girl, was infinitely better than putting a board in front of an open net.

"And one other thing," I added. "You have to get me some proper goalie equipment. I'm not going to stand in front of you guys wearing just shin pads. I want proper goalie pads and mitts and a goalie stick."

"Oh, come on," Malcolm wailed. "That would cost us a ton of money. We can't afford that."

"It's up to you," I said. "Those are my conditions. Take them or leave them."

"We'll take them," Jed conceded.

"Are you crazy?" John said. "Do you know how much goalie equipment costs? It'll be more than the two hundred we're already paying her."

"I think I can get a good deal on some second hand stuff," Jed said. "Won't cost us half as much as new. And we'll have ourselves a real goalie who can maybe stop a puck or two."

"Huh! What makes you so sure she'll be able to stop anything? She's never played goal before. She can hardly skate," Malcolm said.

"Hardly skate!" I yelled. "I can skate better than you can."

Malcolm chuckled. "That'll be the day."

"Besides," I added, "goalies don't need to be great skaters anyway. They just need to be quick. And I'm very quick."

There was a lot of hemming and hawing before they finally agreed to my conditions.

"Okay, we're agreed. I'll see what I can do about getting some equipment. I think it might be best if we don't tell Mom and Dad about our little arrangement. They might not be thrilled with the idea. Best to keep it under our hats."

"They're bound to find out," John said. "How is Katherine going to explain all the new clothes she's suddenly acquired?"

"I can hide them in my room," I suggested. "They'll eventually find out, but maybe by that time it won't matter so much."

"If they make you quit, we get our money back," Malcolm said.

I shook my head. "Not likely. The money would be gone. What would I do? Take back a bunch of used clothes?"

"Oh boy," John wailed, "this is beginning to sound like a really bad situation."

"Hey," Jed said, "think of it as a good investment. We get a goalie for the season, Kat gets lots of practice doing something she otherwise would never do and we get to take some real shots at the goal. Sounds good to me."

"You guys have to promise not to take any slap shots," I said. "I'm not putting my life on the line for a mere 200 bucks."

"A mere 200 bucks!" Jed shook his head. "That sounds pretty generous to me." He sighed and looked around at his brothers. "You know what? I think we're going to have to draw up a contract. Just so we know where we stand. What do you think?"

"That's okay with me," I said. "And if I don't like something in the contract, I have the right to nix it. Right?"

There are a lot of shaking of heads and moaning amongst my brothers, but in the end they agreed and turned back to resume their game.

"I think she should go in goal right now. See if she's any good, as a show of good faith," Malcolm said.

"Good idea," John agreed, looking over at me, knowing full well that I would object. However, considering how generous they were being, I decided to relent. What the heck. The thought of having a shopping spree had put me in a generous mood.

"I'll do it," I said. "But I'll need a pair of shin pads and no raising the puck."

Little did I know that what was about to happen would change my whole outlook on the game of hockey and my place in it.

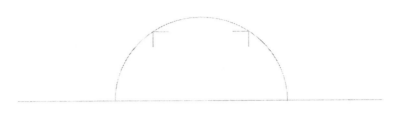

CHAPTER 2

As I mentioned, my brothers are all good hockey players, especially Jed who is older and therefore a little faster and smarter. My expectations as a goalie were, as you can imagine, not very high. After all, I was only fourteen and not very tall and hadn't ever played goalie before. It was all a new experience for me, but as the game progressed, with me donning a pair of shin pads and using a regular hockey stick, I began to really enjoy stopping my big brothers from scoring goals. It was a wonderful way to repay them for all the tormenting they had done over the years. It really wasn't easy being the only girl in a family of five kids. Now, as the goalie, the one position in which I could actually compete against them, I held sway. They had real difficulty scoring on me, which surprised me almost as much as it surprised them.

While I was in goal, the two teams consisting of Malcolm and Jed on one team and Michael and John on the other, didn't use the whole ice surface like they did before. After one team took a shot, they had to carry the puck back over the center line before taking another shot.

With only one goalie, it was a good system and saved me from being peppered constantly. Since they couldn't raise the puck or take slap shots, it made it more challenging for them to score. There was no doubt that I was winning at this new game and I savored it.

I could tell they were getting frustrated and the more frustrated they became, the happier I became. They had promised not to raise the puck, but as the frustration in not being able to score began to get to them, they did just that. A couple of the shots hit me in places with no padding and when that happened, I skated out of the net and the game stopped.

"Hey, what's going on?" Jed wanted to know.

"You guys are raising the puck," I yelled. "You promised you wouldn't."

"What the heck, you stop everything along the ice. What else can we do?" John complained.

"You can't raise the puck until I get goalie equipment," I said. "I could get really hurt and then Mom and Dad would find out."

"Okay, okay, we won't raise it any more. We promise," Jed said, glaring at his brothers. "Come on guys, surely we can beat her by shooting along the ice."

But they weren't able to beat me no matter how hard they tried. I turned them back every time. I was chuckling internally thinking that this business of being a goalie was kind of fun, especially since it involved frustrating my tough, tormenting brothers who were supposed to be such good hockey players.

After nearly an hour and they hadn't scored even one goal, it was time to quit. My brothers didn't even have the grace to congratulate me on my stellar performance.

Jed gave me a pat on the back, but the rest of them just ignored me as though I hadn't done anything special. I could tell their little egos were really bruised. Being shut out by a girl, a fourteen-year-old at that, wasn't something they were going to be bragging about.

It was all I could do not to say anything when we went into the house and my mom asked about our game. The boys were pretty low keyed, muttering under their breath.

"Well aren't you a bunch of grouches," she proclaimed. "I hope you let Katherine share the rink for awhile."

"Oh, she shared it," Jed said, looking over at his brothers. "In fact, she had more than her share."

"Now what is that supposed to mean?" my mother asked, sitting down across from us and giving us that knowing stare she's so famous for.

None of my brothers wanted to answer that one. I mean, what could they say without giving away the fact that I was now not only the recipient of two hundred dollars they were about to fork over, but the object of their frustration. Not to mention that Mom and Dad were not to know that their only daughter was going to be the target of thousands of pucks aimed at her tiny but very quick body over the next few months. Probably something they wouldn't be too thrilled about and might even put the kibosh on.

"Well?" my mother persisted.

"It's nothing...really. We were just having a little shinny game," Jed said. "Nothing special."

Mom didn't look the least bit convinced. "Well, whatever you've been up to, I hope you've been fair to your sister. She's the only one you've got, you know. So treat her right."

I was dying to look over at my brothers, but I didn't dare. I might burst out laughing and then Mom would really be curious. I just looked straight ahead, trying my best not to make Mom any more curious than she already was.

The next morning, we were all up early. My brothers were bound and determined to get their revenge. According to them, my performance the previous day was a fluke. Now it was time to get down to business.

"Are you ready to stop a few pucks?" Jed asked after we had eaten our breakfast and were tying up our skates.

"How about that goalie equipment you are supposed to supply? When do I get that?"

"I'll try to get it today if I can. In the meantime, you're just going to have to wear the shin pads like you did yesterday. It won't hurt you to wear them for one more day."

"Just as long as you don't raise the puck," I countered. "Remember, I'm your only sister."

Jed shook his head. "Yeah, well, little sister, you had better have your A game all ready. It isn't going to be like yesterday. We're going to get serious today, aren't we guys?"

My other brothers noisily agreed by high fiving each other as we all burst out the door in our skates. They were ready to do battle and prove to themselves that their little sister wasn't going to make monkeys out of them again.

Everything started out pretty well. My brothers took several shots at me, all of which I stopped quite easily. Then they each took turns coming in on me, penalty shot style, but not once were they successful. They tried dekeing me, slipping the puck through the five hole, shooting for the corners but I had them figured out every time. By the time they decided to have a little game, they were all pretty frustrated. They were used to scoring at will and now, suddenly, they couldn't even get one goal. What the heck was going on?

Now I have to admit that a couple of times, they did score, but only because one of my brute of a brothers knocked me aside and I fell on my butt. Not exactly fair in my books, but they thought it was pretty cool finally scoring on me.

When we had to quit and get to school, my brothers were a little more chipper than they had been the day before. After all, I hadn't shut them out. They had scored on their so-called invincible sister who was suddenly not so invincible.

Well, I had news for them. Once I got the goalie equipment, those brothers of mine were never, I mean never, going to score on me. And if they got pushy and tried to knock me over, I would threaten to quit. That would get them, especially if I've already had my shopping spree.

Once I got to school, I just had to tell Tracy, my best friend, what had happened with my brothers, but I had to get her to promise not to blab all over the school about it. I didn't want it to get back to my mom and dad. I was enjoying beating my brothers at their own game too much and if Mom and Dad put the kibosh on my playing goal that would ruin everything. Actually, now that I thought about it, I would have played goal for nothing if I had known it was going to be this much fun. Nothing beat frustrating my brothers. They had been a thorn in my side for so many years. Now it was payback time.

"You're playing goalie?" Tracy asked, amazed. "Aren't you afraid of getting hurt?"

Tracy is a very sweet girl, very feminine and pretty and about as far from athletic as you can get. But she's a great friend, very loyal and would do anything for me. The idea of my playing goalie was about as strange to her as my getting a tattoo across my forehead.

"Of course I'm not afraid. They're my brothers and they've promised not to raise the puck or get rowdy with me. Otherwise, I'll threaten to quit."

It then occurred to me that once I got the goalie equipment, they would insist on raising the puck. But maybe then it wouldn't matter. I would have so much protection, the puck would just bounce off me.

"Well, it's your head they'll be shooting at. Better you than me."

I laughed. "They better not be shooting at my head. But if they do, I hope I'll just catch the puck and frustrate them even more."

I then went on to tell Tracy how I had stopped them from scoring, virtually shutting them out. She screamed with delight. She knows my brothers and she could well understand how frustrated they would be.

"Are you really that good?" she asked. "I mean, your brothers are excellent hockey players from what I've heard. I can hardly imagine you stopping them from scoring."

"I don't know. I've never played goalie before in my life. It's like a whole new experience for me. Maybe I'm just talented that way or something. I can't really understand it. But whatever it is, it sure is fun. You should see my brothers. They are so grumpy and the best thing is, they're paying me to play in goal."

"You are kidding," Tracy exclaimed.

"I guess that makes me a professional, huh?" I laughed.

"How much are they paying you for heaven's sake?"

"Would you believe two hundred dollars?"

Tracy shrieked. "Oh my gosh. I can't believe it. Your brothers are giving you two hundred dollars to play in goal. That's absolutely fabulous."

"Now all I have to do is figure out what I want to spend the two hundred dollars on. Any ideas?"

"You've come to the right place," Tracy said. "If there's one thing I'm really good at it's spending money – especially on clothes. So when did you have in mind?"

"How about after school? We could go down to The Bay and see what they've got."

"You mean you've already got the money?"

"Well, no, but there's nothing stopping us from going down and picking out some things. Maybe they've got a layaway plan or something."

Tracy gave me a hug. "I can hardly wait. The Ladies Wear at the Bay will never be the same after you and I have finished with them. This is going to be more exciting than Christmas, Halloween and Thanksgiving all rolled into one."

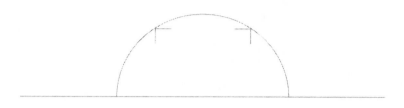

CHAPTER 3

When I got home after my shopping spree with Tracy, during which I easily managed to spend the promised two hundred dollars, Jed was waiting for me in the kitchen. Mom and Dad weren't home yet and Jed looked concerned.

"Where the heck have you been?" he asked. "It's almost 6 o'clock and Mom and Dad'll be home any minute."

I didn't want to admit that I had already spent the two hundred dollars, so I played it coy. I wasn't beyond telling a little white lie. "I had some homework to do at school. What's the big deal?"

"The big deal is that I got the goalie equipment. It cost me more than I thought so the two hundred might have to wait. Anyway, I wanted you to try this stuff on, see where we have to make adjustments. And I wanted to do this before Mom and Dad get home. If they see all this goalie equipment, they're going to wonder what's going on."

The only thing I heard was that the two hundred would have to wait. "Just how long did you have in mind before paying me?" I demanded.

"Hey, what difference does it make? You'll get your money. Those brothers of yours are so cheap, it might take a while to squeeze anything out of them."

"I've got obligations," I explained. "I need that two hundred soon, like real soon."

Jed ignored my plea and headed for the door. "I've got the goalie equipment out in the garage. "Let's go and see how it fits."

I reluctantly followed him, thinking all the time about when I was going to get paid. Knowing my brothers, they would do their best to squirm out of it somehow, but I wasn't going to let them get away with it, especially the twins who hung on to their money like their lives depended on it. Besides, I had over two hundred dollars worth of clothes that I was dying to wear waiting for me at the Bay.

It was cold in the shed so Jed turned on the heat. "I got pretty much everything you'll need," he explained, hauling out the equipment from the back of his car. "Here, try these on."

He handed me shoulder pads and a chest protector that looked big enough for a Sumo wrestler. I couldn't help but laugh. "You expect me to wear that!" I exclaimed.

"Of course," Jed said. "It'll protect your...your chest and your stomach. You know, your mid-section."

"But it's too big," I said, trying my best to wrap it around myself.

Jed took the ends of it and pulled it tight. "It just needs to be tied, that's all. There, it's perfect."

I felt like I was in a straight jacket. How was I even going to be able to move, let alone stop a puck? At least the shoulder pads seemed to fit all right.

"You said you wouldn't take any slap shots," I reminded him.

"Are you kidding? That was before you got all this equipment. The puck will just bounce off you. It won't hurt at all." He handed me the goalie gloves. "You're good at baseball so you'll easily be able to catch the puck with these."

I tried the gloves on. They were large too, way too large for my little hands. But I might be able to get used to them.

Next came the goalie pants and then the goalie pads. They were truly large but surprisingly light. Jed helped me strap them on and I couldn't help but laugh. I must look like a new species of animal, I thought. Thank heavens none of my friends would be around to see me dressed up in this stuff. They would never let me forget how funny I looked.

Next came the elbow pads that covered almost my entire arms and finally the mask. A large, fierce-looking eagle was painted on the front. It was really cool. It was too big too, but we were able to make some adjustments so that it fit reasonably well.

Last came the goalie stick. Wow! With that in my hand, my brothers were never going to score on me. It was so much better than a regular hockey stick. Again, it was too big for me, but cutting it down to my size wouldn't be that difficult.

"So what do you think?" Jed asked, looking at me and trying his best not to laugh. I must have looked pretty funny. Moving around with all this stuff on me was going to take some getting used to.

"I feel like an astronaut getting ready for takeoff," I said. "Do I look as comical as I feel?"

"You look...great," Jed smiled broadly. "Like a real pro."

What a liar, I thought. He's having a good laugh at my expense, but I would have the last laugh when we got on the ice. If my brothers were frustrated before I got this equipment, it was nothing to what they were about to experience now.

The next morning, I got my first opportunity to try out my new equipment. My brothers just gaped when they saw me leave the garage and skate onto the ice. I must have been quite a sight with Jed's oversized sweater hanging down almost to my knees. I tried my best to act as though nothing was out of the ordinary, but it was a little difficult with my brothers hooting and hollering. I guess they thought I looked pretty funny and I probably did, but I had already accepted that fact. It didn't matter how funny I looked as long as I could stop my brothers from scoring goals.

For the first few minutes, my brothers lined up on the blue line and shot a few pucks at me and I didn't have any trouble turning them aside. The goalie stick was so much better than an ordinary stick, but it was a little clumsy at first. Once I got used to it, I would be much better at stopping pucks. This was turning out to be a lot more fun than I expected.

Once the game started, things got a little dicier. My brothers were throwing everything they could at me and were determined not to be shut out like they had been the previous day. They did manage to get a few pucks past me, but I chalked it up to the new equipment. I knew that once I got used to it, my brothers were going to be very disappointed. Their little egos were going to be very badly bruised.

"Hey little sister, you're doing great," Jed said after we had finished and I had shucked off the goalie equipment. "You got real talent girl. You're better than our goalie, and he's supposed to be the best around here. In fact, he's hoping to get a scholarship next year to the University of Denver."

I couldn't help laughing. "You're kidding. I'm better than Kyle Gooding?"

"You are. There's no doubt about it in my mind. Wow! Maybe you'll be able to get a scholarship some day. If you keep this up, I'd say your chances are pretty good. There's lots of women's hockey teams in the U.S."

"I want to play against the men," I declared. "Playing against girls would be too easy."

Jed laughed. "Let's not get too carried away. Playing against guys won't be easy. Being a good goaltender doesn't involve just stopping pucks. Some of these guys get pretty rough and they're big and strong. They love to knock you over, trip you up, anything to score a goal. And they won't care whether you are a girl or a guy."

"Well, I'm only fourteen. By the time I'm ready for a scholarship, I'll be a lot bigger and feistier."

That night, Jed asked me if I wanted to come into town with him and watch his team, the Centennials, practice. It would give me a good opportunity to study their two goalies and maybe pick up a few hints.

"You don't have to ask me that twice," I said. "I'd love to."

It wasn't the first time that I had seen Jed playing hockey. I had been to a few of his games, but I hadn't paid much attention to the goalies. They were just these big blobs stopping pucks and I hadn't thought about what went into being a goalie. Now things were different. I could compare myself to them. What moves would they make, what things would they do that I wasn't doing? The very thought sent a thrill through my whole body. I couldn't wait.

There were only a few people in the stands, most of them relatives of the players. I sat huddling under a heat lamp, watching Jed's team skating around and around the rink as they warmed up for their practice. Even the goalies skated along with the rest of the players. Both goalies were excellent skaters which surprised me. Maybe I wasn't quite as good as I thought I was. They could both skate better than I could. Guess I was going to have to do a little practice in that area.

The most interesting part of their practice was when they lined up a lot of pucks on the blue line and peppered the goalies with shot after shot. The goalies easily handled the pucks, picking some of them off with their gloves and knocking them aside with their sticks. I was impressed. What I wouldn't do to be out there in full gear. I was more anxious than ever to show off my new-found talent.

I chattered all the way home to Jed about his practice and how much I liked it. He didn't say much. He probably thought I was becoming a real pain talking non-stop the way I was. But I knew he was proud of me. Not like my other brothers who just thought of me as a competitor or someone to tease. Jed was on my side, thank heavens. I really needed his support.

I didn't tell him that I thought I could do almost as well as his goalies. That would have sounded a little too much like I was bragging or something. But I knew that I could compete, that I was pretty good, maybe even good enough to play Juvenile in a few years.

When we got home, Mom seemed a little concerned. I guess she was wondering why I was going to Jed's hockey practice. She probably thought I was secretly meeting some boy or something.

"Have you got all your homework done?" she asked, shortly after I arrived.

"I did it after school," I said.

After I had hung up my coat and got a drink from the fridge, Mom said, "I want to talk to you for a minute."

I looked over at her. She had this funny look on her face, kind of serious like. I wondered what was up because it isn't often Mom wants to talk to me like this, especially looking so serious. What had I done now? I really had finished my homework at school and I was getting A's in almost everything. It couldn't be about school.

"I don't like you going out on a school night," she said, once we were settled on the couch. "If I had been home I wouldn't have let you go."

"I just went to see Jed's hockey practice. All I did was sit in the stands and watch."

"I know. That's not what's bothering me. I just don't think a fourteen-year-old girl should be going out during the week, especially to a cold old arena. There's no telling who's hanging around there. And if anything happened, Jed wouldn't be able to help you. He would be too bound up in his practice to even notice."

"What could possibly happen to me in an arena, Mom? There's other people around, most of them parents."

"And you just went to see how your brother was making out?" She shook her head. "I think I know why the sudden interest in your brother's hockey practice."

'You do?" I was shocked. Did she think I had a crush on one of the players?

"There's not much around here I'm not aware of," she continued. "I know you've been playing goaltender for the boys and I don't like it. You could get hurt. They're much bigger than you and much rougher. I don't want my little girl hurt by a flying puck in the mouth."

"Mom, I've got a mask to protect my face. But, how did you know I was playing in goal? I suppose one of the twins told you. They are really bummed out because they haven't been able to score on me. This is their way of getting rid of me and the..." Whoops! I was going to mention the money they owed me but managed to stop myself in time. No use getting Mom more upset than she already was.

"Nobody told me. I'm usually pretty aware of what's going on in my own house. Let's leave it at that."

"Mom, I really like playing in goal. It's so much fun and I think I'm really good at it."

"I'm surprised you haven't already got some bumps and bruises. What possessed you to do this?"

Well, I couldn't exactly tell her that I was bribed, that the promised 200 dollars was the real incentive and not the love of the game. "I...I just thought it might be fun, that's all. And it is. Don't make me quit, please."

My mother shook her head. "I can't imagine why you want to do this. It's a rough game. It's not a game for a girl."

"Mom, there are lots of women's teams all over the country. They play in the Olympics. Women have been playing hockey for a long time."

"But they aren't playing against men. They're playing against other women, aren't they?"

I didn't have an answer for that one. "The boys have promised to take it easy on me," I said. "After all, I'm their sister. They won't get rough with me." What was I saying? Did I really believe that? Not on your life. My brothers would do almost anything to score a goal on me, except maybe Jed who had a little more common sense.

"I'll have a talk to them," Mom said.

"Does that mean I can still play goalie?" I asked.

Mom didn't say anything for a few minutes. She just looked off into the distance, as though trying to make up her mind. "You really want to do this?" she finally asked, looking incredulous.

"I do. More than anything. More than play the piano even. I think I've found something that is really challenging, something I can do really well."

Mom shook her head. "I must be crazy, but okay, as long as the boys agree to not play rough and not shoot too hard at you. And as long as your dad approves."

I reached over and gave my mom a huge hug. "Thanks Mom. You'll see. Things are going to turn out real well. I'm going to make you proud."

"I'm already proud of you, dear. You don't have to become a goalie to make me proud if that's why you're doing it."

"It's not," I assured her. It was to make my brothers squirm when they couldn't score on me, especially the twins. And also because I could do it and do it well. And, of course, there was that 200 dollars.

As Mom was about to leave the room, she turned and asked: "Are the boys really having a hard time scoring on you?"

I nodded my head vigorously. "They are, and it's going to get worse for them," I said. "They haven't seen anything yet."

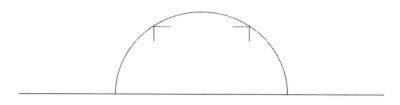

CHAPTER 4

During the next week I continued to frustrate my brothers by stopping almost all of their shots. They tried everything to score on me. They would come in full bore and try to deke me but I was onto them and knew what they were going to do even before they did it. I covered the angles well and didn't give them much to shoot at. They even tried to do spineramas, but that didn't work for them either.

"It would be different if we were playing a real game, Malcolm complained. "Anybody can stop a few pucks, especially if you're not screened and nobody's hassling you."

"Hey little brother," Jed said. "Give your sister her due. She's doing really well and being a good sport about it. Stop complaining and making excuses."

"Yeah, and I haven't seen any money yet," I rejoined. "When am I going to see some green?"

"It shouldn't be too long now," Jed said. "I get paid on Saturday. Maybe we can settle up then. What do you say guys?"

The twins had suddenly become deaf. It was amazing how they couldn't hear stuff they didn't want to hear.

"How much is this costing us anyhow?" Michael said.

"I thought we had all this worked out long ago," I replied. "Surely thirty-five dollars isn't going to break you guys and look what you're getting for your money."

"Yeah," John said. "The opportunity to shoot pucks into those big pads of yours. Where did you get those anyway? They look a lot bigger than most goalie pads."

I couldn't help but laugh. "They only look big, stupid, because I'm smaller than most of the goalies you guys face. But I think I'm a little quicker, wouldn't you agree?"

"No I wouldn't," Malcolm said. "You're just...lucky or something."

"Boy, what a couple of poor sports, "I said. "Can't score any goals so you blame the goalie. Not very cool." I loved baiting my brothers. It wasn't very often that I could get the better of them at anything. Suddenly all that was changed. I was getting them where they lived and loving it.

"Saturday is the deadline," I pronounced. "After that, if I don't get the money, I'm withdrawing my services." It was an empty threat and I knew it. I didn't want to stop playing goal and would have done it for nothing, but a deal was a deal and I wasn't going to let them off the hook if I could help it.

"You'll get it," Jed said. "I'll make sure of it." He glared at his brothers. "Now let's get back to playing a little hockey."

A couple of weeks later, Jed's hockey coach appeared at our door one evening. When Mom answered, she was surprised to see Eric Sanderson standing on the doorstep.

"Hi Eric," she welcomed him. "Come on in. Jed is up in his room doing his homework. I'll just give him a holler."

"Actually, I came to see Katherine. Could I talk to her for a minute?"

"Katherine? Oh, sure. Just a minute."

I was in the kitchen and could hear them talking. What in the world did Coach Sanderson want with me?

When I appeared, he smiled. "Hi there, Katherine. Hope I'm not taking you away from anything."

"No, I was just tidying up in the kitchen."

I must have looked a little dumbfounded as he laughed. "You're probably wondering what I'm doing here."

"Why don't you come in and sit down," my mother said, leading him toward the living room. "It's a little more comfortable than standing here in the hallway."

After we were all seated, Coach Sanderson looked over at me. "I hear you're a pretty good goalie. Jed tells me your brothers are having a hard time scoring on you."

"They are," I admitted. "And they're not happy about it either."

"I would like to see you play sometime," he said. "One of our goalies, maybe you know him, Kyle Gooding, well, he broke his ankle skiing last weekend, so we're looking for a replacement."

"And you want me to play for the Centennials in his place?"

"Well, only if you want to and if you're up to it and your parents don't object. That's why I would like to see you in action, see if you could do it or not."

My mother looked over at me and then at Coach Sanderson. "Katherine's only fourteen and in the ninth grade. I don't think she's ready for anything like you're suggesting."

" Actually, we only need her as a backup until Kyle gets back. If she's as good as Jed says, she could help our team a lot. We wouldn't put her in any games or anything, but it would be good practice for her and help us out at the same time."

"Can I, Mom? I'm already facing those brothers of mine. It's not as though it would be something I haven't done before. I think I'm ready."

"Katherine, this is...ridiculous. Playing with your brothers is one thing, but..."

Jed entered the room and sat down across from his coach. "Everything okay?" he asked, winking at his coach and smiling over at my mother.

"I can see you had something to do with this," my mother said accusingly. "Do you really think Katherine is ready to play goal against a bunch of ruffians?"

"They're all nice guys, Mom. Really. Besides, I don't see why me and my brothers should be the only ones blanked by that sister of mine. And yes, I think she could do it."

"Would the team allow a girl to play with the boys?" Mom wanted to know.

"I've already asked our sponsors about that," Coach Sanderson stated. "And they have no objections as long as you give your permission. Also, I put it to the team as well and some of them were pretty surprised and one or two thought she might have a rough time of it. But most didn't raise any objections. I think the doubters will change their minds pretty quickly once they see her in action."

"You've certainly gone to a lot of trouble," my mom said. "You must want her to play pretty badly."

"We do. Good goaltenders are hard to find. But I would have to see how she plays first."

"We practice every morning before school," Jed said. "Can you make it out around seven tomorrow morning?"

"Absolutely," Coach Sanderson smiled over at me. "I'll see you in the morning then." As he turned toward the door, he stopped. "I'm looking forward to this. It isn't every day that I get to audition a goaltender, especially of the female persuasion."

After he had gone, my mother glared at Jed. "You could have told me," she accused. "I don't like surprises, especially about my daughter."

"Sorry, Mom. I thought you would probably say no, I guess. But I'll keep an eye on her. I promise."

I didn't sleep much that night thinking about my "audition" the next morning. Playing on the same team as Jed was going to be a blast, provided, of course, that Coach Sanderson liked how I played. But I really wasn't worried about that. I had a lot of confidence in my performance as a goaltender. I was quite sure that if I could stop my brothers from scoring, I wouldn't have much difficulty with any other players. After all, my brothers were all accomplished players and usually were the leading scorers on their teams.

As I skated out onto the ice the next morning, I could see Coach Sanderson's car pulling into our driveway. He was right on time.

Jed started peppering me with shots and as usual, I knocked them aside. By the time Coach Sanderson arrived at our rink, I was beginning to hit my stride.

"Good morning," he yelled, leaning on the boards and looking over at us. "Nice little setup you've got here."

"You can thank my dad," Jed said. "He built it and keeps it maintained. We try to help out as much as we can."

No sooner were those words out of Jed's mouth when my Dad appeared. He shook hands with Coach Sanderson. "How are you doing, Eric?" he asked. "Nice of you to come out so early."

The two men were such a contrast, I had to smile. Whereas my dad was tall and muscular, Coach Sanderson was quite stocky and short. They already knew each other well and were about the same age.

"Jed tells me Katherine's quite the goalie," Coach Sanderson said. "I thought I would come out and see for myself."

My dad looked over at me. "Well, she's pretty feisty if that helps in being a goalie and I suspect it does."

The twins and Michael appeared and skated onto the ice. They looked sullen as though they were afraid that I was going to make them look bad. And I was hoping to do just that, but my main concern was to impress the coach.

My brothers lined up on the blue line and began shooting pucks at me. I handled them without difficulty. It didn't matter to me whether they were slap shots or just wrist shots. I was getting used to the heavy equipment and I felt I could use the goalie stick much better now that I was used to it being heavier and bulkier than an ordinary stick. Jed had cut it down quite a bit to suit my small frame.

The next exercise my brothers did was line rushes. They would come in on me two at a time, passing the puck and trying to get me to commit myself and then throw the puck into the open net. But they were seldom successful, and I managed to turn them back time after time.

We always ended our sessions with a scrimmage. It was my favorite part of the practice as it simulated a real game situation and gave me an opportunity to show off what I could do.

When we finally skated off the ice, Coach Sanderson approached me. "Wow!" he declared. "You were sensational. I've never seen anybody your age, boy or girl, play goal like that. How long have you been doing it?"

"Only a short while," I said excitedly. I looked over at Dad. He was looking about as proud as any parent could look.

"She's something else, isn't she? And I'm not just saying that because she's my daughter. She really is exceptional."

"Indeed she is and I would be honored if you would consider joining our team, Katherine," Coach said. He turned to my dad. "If it's okay with you, that is."

"If it's what she wants," Dad said.

"It's what I want," I said firmly. "I love being a goalie. It's a lot of fun and I think I can do it really well."

"From what I've seen this morning," the coach said, "I would guess you're going to do all right. Better than all right actually. I think those young guys on my team are about to get the surprise of their young lives."

Dad looked at his watch. "I've got to get to work." He ruffled my hair. "Never thought I would have a tomboy for a daughter," he said. "All my sisters were proper young ladies who liked dolls, shopping and the like. I couldn't imagine any of them wanting to be a goalie."

"I'm not a tomboy," I countered, remembering all the clothes that were still at the Bay waiting for me to pick them up. "I just like playing in goal. It's very satisfying to be good at something that most other girls would find really strange."

As I watched Coach Sanderson drive away, I felt a wonderful sense of well being. To have him come all the way out here just to see me was a thrill in itself, but to have him say that I was sensational. Well, that was something I would remember for a long time.

As Jed drove us into town the next night, I was jittery and couldn't stop talking. As hard as I tried I couldn't seem to get a word out of him. He seemed strangely quiet. Maybe, I thought, he was regretting telling his coach about me. Maybe the thought of having his little sister on the same team wasn't sitting too well with him.

When we got to the arena and were about to enter the dressing room, it suddenly occurred to me that I couldn't very well go into a room with a bunch of half-dressed guys. What should I do?

"You can get dressed in the ladies rest room over there," Jed said, pointing to a sign that read WOMEN.

I was doing my best to drag all my goalie equipment which weighed almost as much as I did. I opened the door to the restroom and pulled my equipment bag in behind me. There wasn't a lot of room and nowhere to sit down, but I managed after several minutes of trying to find a suitable place to change, to struggle into my goalie equipment and head out to the ice surface.

Most of the players were already skating around, passing a puck and generally warming up. I felt a little strange, until Iggy Johnson came up to me and welcomed me to the team. He was the backup goalie.

"I thought coach was kidding when he told us about you," he said. "We don't see too many girl goalies these days."

"I hope I can help the team," I said, not knowing what else to say. Iggy was a good friend of Jed and was a couple of grades ahead of me at school. He was also big, over 6 feet and probably weighed almost 200 pounds.

A few minutes later, Coach Sanderson skated onto the ice and blew his whistle. All the players crowded around him and he introduced me to the team. "Katherine is going to help us out for a while until Kyle gets back. I want you guys to take it easy on her. She's new to this and so I expect you won't try anything funny or be unnecessarily rough. Does everybody understand that?"

There was a general nodding of heads amongst the players.

"Okay, let's do some sprints and stops and starts."

We all lined up at one end and at the whistle, everybody skated as hard as they could until coach blew the whistle. Then we put on the brakes until he blew the whistle again. We did that for about five minutes, and I was so out of breath, I could barely stand up.

"You'll get used to it," Iggy said. "It's harder for us because we're carrying a whole lot more weight than the other players."

When I finally had the opportunity to stop a few pucks, I was relieved. It was quite obvious that I was sadly out of shape. I was going to have to do some work in that area if I was going to be able to compete.

At first the players were a little confused about what to do with this new goaltender. Some seemed a little hostile and made rude comments when they skated by me, but I did my best to ignore them. They weren't quite sure what coach meant when he had said to take it easy on me, so they did just that. Their shots were mostly along the ice and without much force and I had no trouble stopping them. When they did line rushes, I had no trouble stopping all their shots and I think it shocked them a little. I could see some of them shaking their heads as though wondering what was going on. How was it possible that this little grade 9 girl was stopping all their shots?

As the practice went on, they began to shoot harder, but I didn't mind. I was used to my brothers shooting as hard as they could, so it was nothing new. I really enjoyed it when they lined up on the blue line and peppered me with shots. I was proud of the way I was able to stop all their shots either by catching them or knocking them aside with my goalie stick.

At the end of the practice, a lot of the players came over to me and complimented me on my performance after banging their sticks against my pads.

"I'm sure glad you're on our side," one of them said.

"I think our opposition's in for a big surprise," another said.

Coach came over and took me aside. "That was great, Katherine. The guys are impressed. I just hope they can get used to not scoring too many goals in practice."

"I had a ball. It was really a lot of fun, but I'm not in very good shape. Guess I'll have to start doing some wind sprints or something."

"Don't worry about it too much and whatever you do, don't overdo it. I don't want you to get injured. We need you healthy."

On the way home, Jed was much more talkative than he had been on the way in.

"You did really well, Kat. Nice going. The guys thought you were really something and coach is over the moon. I guess he thinks he's got a secret weapon now."

"I'm just supposed to be a backup, right? I won't be playing in any games, will I?"

Jed laughed. "Well, don't tell Mom, but I'm betting coach is going to have you in goal sooner than you might expect."

"Really?" I said excitedly.

"Really," Jed said.

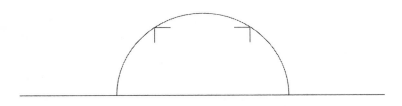

CHAPTER 5

The next few weeks were very exciting for me. I was enjoying the practices with the team and also got a lot of satisfaction out of frustrating my brothers, especially the twins. They thought they were God's gift to the hockey world, but now they were having to do a little reassessment. After all, if you couldn't score on your little sister, how could you consider yourself a hot-shot hockey player?

Sometimes I could hear them complaining to Mom about it. Girls were supposed to do girl things, they complained. It wasn't fair that she was playing a man's game and making them look bad. It seemed like everybody was talking about her and how wonderful she was. It was bad enough having a sister who was always getting in your hair and contradicting you, but now she was turning into a real pain.

"You should be proud of her," my mother said. "She's doing something very few girls can do, and doing it better than most boys could. Give her credit and stop your whining."

"Yeah but she's always–"

"I don't want to hear any more about it."

I had to smile thinking about my brothers having to swallow their pride. They were such poor sports at times, and were so eager to have my parents' approval that they would do almost anything to get their attention. I felt a little sorry for them sometimes. And besides, they still hadn't coughed up their part of the 200 dollars they owed me. Jed and Michael had both given me part of the money and the twins grudgingly said they would pay me when they could, whenever that would be. I wasn't going to hold my breath. I had almost enough to pay for the clothes that I had bought at the Bay, so even if they never paid me, I could add some of my own money and pick up the clothes the Bay was holding for me.

About a week after I started playing with Jed's team, the coach told me we were going to have a game against another team that the Centennials hadn't beaten for several seasons. They were from Summerville, a town about forty miles away, called themselves the Nighthawks and they had several really good players who especially loved playing us mainly because they knew they could kick our butts. The two teams had had a long standing rivalry over the years, but for some reason, they were having a long run of victories against us.

Coach talked to us about their team at length one night after practice.

"They're big and they're mean," he said, "and they've got all the confidence in the world. If we're going to beat them, we're just going to have to outsmart them."

"How do we do that?" one of the players asked.

"By keeping the puck out of our end, doing lots of fore checking, and beating them to the puck whenever we can.

I think we're faster than they are and if we play smarter, that gives us at least a chance to beat them. And we can't afford to take penalties. I know how frustrated you guys get sometimes, but retaliating doesn't help anybody. It just gets us in penalty trouble."

Coach told me later that I would be the backup goalie. He had no intentions of playing me, he said, but he had to have another goalie on hand just in case.

I was excited. I had never played in a real hockey game in my entire life. What would it be like to be right there in the middle of the action? And what if Iggy got hurt? I would be in the game, wouldn't I? The very thought set my heart ticking wildly. Would I be able to stop their shots like I stopped our own players' shots? Maybe they would get rough with me, try to knock me off my feet. Well, just let them try it. I wasn't going to be any kind of pushover if I had anything to say about it.

I thought about the upcoming game the whole week. Sometimes I couldn't get to sleep at night thinking about it. Jed said that it was no big deal. He figured we could beat them. And then he said something really sweet.

"I figure if you were in goal, those Nighthawks wouldn't have a prayer."

"Do you really mean that?" I asked him.

"Of course I mean it. You've already shown that you can keep our guys from scoring most of the time. There's no reason why you can't stop them." He started to laugh, looking over at me as we drove back home.

"What's so funny?" I asked.

"I was just thinking about the twins. They're really twisting in the wind because they can't score on you. Wait till some of those Nighthawks get a load of you. They are going to be feeling worse than the twins."

"I don't think that's possible," I said, chuckling. "They hardly even speak to me anymore and when they do, it's to say something sarcastic."

"They'll get over it. Their egos are suffering a little, that's all. Once they accept the fact that you're really good and nobody else is scoring goals against you, they'll straighten up."

The game against the Nighthawks turned out to be a fizzle. They were really good and beat us soundly 8 to 1. I sat on the bench hoping against hope that I might get into the game for a little while, but with Mom and Dad sitting up in the stands, the coach didn't even look my way. Iggy didn't have one of his best games and let in a few softies that I was sure I would have stopped, but since the game was out of hand early, I guess the coach figured there wasn't much chance of winning even if I went in goal.

"It's okay guys," Coach said after the game. "We had a bad night. It happens sometimes. We'll get them next time."

I'm not sure anybody believed it. They were bigger and more aggressive than we were and had the confidence that they could beat us any time they wanted. Our team looked disheartened as I glanced along the bench at them. They needed to be fired up. Even Jed looked discouraged.

Iggy came up to me after the game shaking his head. "You should go in next time," he said. "I was terrible tonight. I don't think I could have stopped a football."

"I thought you did pretty well," I told him, "except for maybe a couple of goals at the beginning."

All the way home, Jed couldn't stop talking about the game and how badly they had played. "It's always the same thing," he said. "They get a few goals up on us and then we just collapse. It's the story of our life." He looked over at me. "We got to get you in goal. I think then we would have a chance. Iggy just didn't do the job tonight, especially early when we needed to keep even with them."

"Coach said I was just going to be a practice goalie, that I wouldn't be playing in any games."

Jed shook his head. "Well, we're just going to have to work on him, aren't we? Convince him otherwise."

"What about Mom?" I asked. "Coach more or less promised her I wouldn't be playing in any games. He won't want to go back on his word, will he?"

"Maybe we can talk to Mom, try to get her to understand the situation. You have to get into a game sooner or later. I didn't buy all that equipment so you could sit on the bench."

"Thanks Jed. You've been great. I just hope Mom doesn't pop a blood vessel when we try to get her to let me play in a game."

"Well, we have to wait and see what Coach has to say. I have a feeling the next time we play the Nighthawks, he'll want you in goal."

When we got home, Mom and Dad were there. Neither of them said much and I was dying to ask Mom about my going into a game, but I knew it was premature. First off, Coach hadn't even asked me, and besides, Mom probably assumed that I was just a backup and wouldn't be playing anyway. There was just no way she was going to let her precious little daughter be the target of a rowdy bunch of juveniles who unleashed slap shots that could put a hole in a wall.

"You guys were pretty bad tonight," my dad said to Jed. "You let those guys run roughshod over you. You need to be a little tougher, do a little more back checking. And I think you need Katherine in goal. That guy Iggy let too many easy ones get by him."

Jed and I looked at one another in shock and then over at Mom. She was looking at Dad with daggers in her eyes.

"Frank! Where did that come from? I thought we agreed that Katherine would only be a back up until Kyle comes back?"

Dad looked a little befuddled. "Well, it's obvious they need her. I don't think they'll even be able to give the Nighthawks a game while Iggy's playing goal and Kyle might not be back for the rest of the season."

"Katherine's too young," Mom said. "She'll get hurt. Some of those Nighthawks were twice her size and did you see some of the shots they took on poor old Iggy? I don't want my daughter facing that kind of...of barrage."

"Apparently it's what she wants," Dad said. He looked over at me. "Danged if I can figure it out, but hey, if she wants to be a goalie, let's let her be a goalie."

"I want to do it," I said. "I really do. More than anything."

Mom sat glaring at my Dad for several minutes. "I can't believe you're willing to let your daughter be the target of a bunch of hard-shooting hockey goons. Those pucks can do a lot of damage. Not to mention if they run into her and knock her over."

My dad laughed. "Have you seen the equipment she's wearing? There's hardly a square inch of her little body that isn't protected. She's probably safer in goal than she is riding in the car."

"Nice try," my mom said. She still looked unconvinced.

"She hasn't been hurt yet," Jed said, "and we've been shooting at her for almost a month. And I think I can shoot as hard as any of the Nighthawks."

Mom still didn't look convinced as she rose and started up the stairs mumbling something about why she couldn't have had a daughter who was content to do girl things.

Dad shrugged. "I'll talk to her," he said to me. "She'll come around."

I could hardly believe my luck. Was it possible that I might be in goal sooner than I thought? I smiled over at Jed. Now all we had to do was hope Coach would suggest that I play goal in the next game.

The next few weeks were pretty quiet. Mom hadn't said anything since that night and my brothers seemed to enjoy peppering me with shots. I think I was still frustrating them a little. I had derived a little scheme whereby I let a few pucks get by me. It seemed to satisfy the twins somewhat. At least they weren't entirely shut out by their little sister. Jed's team practiced twice a week and played a game at least once a week. Coach still hadn't put me into a game, but I hadn't really expected him to when we just played local teams. We didn't have that much trouble beating most of the other teams we played. It was just the Nighthawks that seemed to have our number.

I was surprised when one night Mom decided to have a family meeting. We hadn't had one of those since I was about 12. What could it be about? As far as I could see, everything was going along pretty well in our family. We all got along...sort of.

But one night, there we all were, sitting around the living room table, my Mom sitting at the head looking about as serious as I've ever seen her look. I was beginning to get a little nervous. Was this the beginning of the end of my goalie career?

"I called this meeting," my mom said, "to clear the air a little bit. I'm a little upset over what's happening amongst you kids." She looked at me and then over at the twins. "It would seem John and Malcolm, that you are constantly complaining about Katherine. I'm not sure why. It seems to me that you guys should be supporting your sister instead of complaining about her all the time. After all, she is doing something quite extraordinary in my view."

When nobody said anything, she added: "And Katherine, you aren't helping things by baiting your brothers. It would help if you could...well, tone it down a little at times."

"She's such a prima donna," Malcolm said all of a sudden. "She thinks she's so good just because she's a goalie. And she's always trying to make us look bad."

"Yeah, and everything is about HER," John added. "You would think she was the only person in this family. Just because she thinks she's such a hot goalie, doesn't make her anything special. All the rest of us play hockey too. How come she's so special?"

"You guys are so lame," Jed said. "Give me a break. You're just mad because you can't score on her. If you guys were scoring at will, you'd be running around her like a couple of wild animals taunting her and giving her a bad time. I think it's time you grew up and accepted the fact that Kat is something special. She's got a real talent."

My dad sat at the end of the table with his arms folded. "I can't believe what I'm hearing. We're supposed to be a family. That means we support each other. Jealousy and hard feelings don't have any place in our family. We all need to pull together, stand together no matter what. Petty jealousies, bickering, name-calling, sarcasm. As far as I'm concerned, if I hear that kind of stuff, none of you are going to be playing hockey."

There was a long silence during which my brothers looked down at the table. Michael looked over at me and smiled. I almost fell off my chair. He had been anything but encouraging until now and almost always sided with the twins.

"I think she's great," he admitted. "Some of the guys I play with told me they thought she was the best goalie they had ever seen. I felt pretty proud of her when I heard that."

The twins glared at Michael. He smiled back at them and shrugged. "She's really good. Everybody at school is talking about her."

"My second reason for calling this meeting is about the money the boys paid you," Mom said, looking at me and then at her sons. "I don't know what you boys were thinking about, but nobody is going to pay Kat for playing goalie. As far as I'm concerned, that's bribery and not acceptable. It's quite obvious that Kat enjoys playing in goal without being paid for it. So I expect you to return the money to the boys, Kat. And the sooner the better."

I shrugged, glad that I still hadn't picked up the clothes at the Bay. It would have been a little difficult to return the clothes if I had bought them and worn them. And how did Mom know about our little arrangement anyway? Did one of the twins tell her? I was dying to know, but didn't dare ask. That might be like poking at a hornet's nest. Best to leave it alone.

"Okay," I said. "The twins didn't give me any money anyway, so I don't owe them anything."

"We hadn't intended to–" Malcolm looked over at his dad who was glaring at him. He shrugged and looked down at the table. "Is the meeting over?" he asked.

"Only if you're willing to accept my terms," Dad said. "No more bickering and complaining. Have I got your word?"

The twins looked at each other and then back at their dad. "I guess," Malcolm said.

"Well, I hope you mean that," Dad said. "Otherwise, you know the consequences."

When everybody had left, Mom patted the seat beside her. "I want to talk to you for a minute," she said.

Oh, oh, now what? Was she going to try and talk me out of playing goal? Hadn't she just about given her consent to my playing in a game? I sat down beside her and she put her arm around me.

"I'm a little worried about something," she said. When I gave her my best doe-eyed look, she continued. "It's wonderful that you are so confident about your goal tending and that you know that you are very good at it. Having confidence is a nice thing and something we all need if we're going to succeed at whatever we take on. But sometimes the line between being confident and being cocky is a very fine one. Not that I think you are cocky, I don't, but I think the twins do. They don't have your kind of confidence and when they see you doing so well in goal and then vocalizing it, they see that as bragging. They don't see it the same way you and I see it."

"So you want me to...what? Not talk about my goal-tending in front of them so I can preserve their delicate little egos?"

Mom laughed. "I wouldn't put it quite so bluntly, dear, but yes, tone it down a bit and give them a little latitude. I'm sure once they get used to the fact that you are very good, they'll eventually accept it without being envious."

"Okay," I said. "It won't be easy, but I'll try my best."

Mom gave me a hug. "I knew I could count on you. Now it's time to do your homework. Did you practice the piano today?"

"Yeah, for a little while. I'm still having trouble with that one piece."

"Well, don't forget – playing hockey isn't the be all and end all of everything. You've got a lot of other things on your plate."

Didn't I know it.

The next morning, we practiced as usual and things went better than I expected. Nobody said anything insulting. We simply concentrated on playing hockey and trying to improve our games. When I got to school, I told Tracy about having to return the money and we both went downtown to the Bay after school and explained everything to the lady who had put the clothes away for me. She was sympathetic and said it was no big deal. It wasn't easy saying goodbye to all those nice new clothes, but what the heck. Maybe the twins would turn over a new leaf and start acting like brothers instead of opponents. That would be worth more than having a bunch of new dresses.

Tracey seemed a little upset about something and when I asked her about it, she said that she was concerned about all the hockey I was playing and that we never seemed to spend much time together any more. I tried to cheer her up and reassure her that she was still my best friend and that I would do my best to find some time for us. I'm not sure she was very convinced, but at least I got a smile out of her and she was more cheerful after that.

School seemed to drag that day. I could hardly wait until 7 o'clock when our practice started. It would be interesting to see what Coach would say and whether he would suggest I go in goal the next time we played the Nighthawks. Of course, if he didn't, I would just have to be patient and prove to him that I was good enough.

Jed was in good humor when I got home. He too was looking forward to practice that night. "It's really great having you on the team," he said. "I wonder how many other guys have a sister who's playing on the same team. Maybe we're the only ones in the whole world."

"I don't know any other girls who play hockey, let alone in goal. I know there's lots of girl's hockey around, but I've never seen any of them play except on T.V."

Around the supper table, Dad started kidding me about what I might have to do to improve my goal tending like lifting weights and becoming muscle-bound and eating lots of meat to get enough energy. Mom wasn't amused. My brothers were all smiles.

The practice that night was really heated. Coach had us doing wind sprints and skating hard the whole practice. By the time it ended, I was really beat. What the other players didn't realize was that practicing with all that goalie equipment on was really hard. I probably weighed about twice as much when I was fully dressed. It certainly felt it anyway.

Getting dressed and undressed in the ladies restroom was becoming a problem. It was really small and didn't exactly smell wonderful. And besides, if I was going to bond with the rest of the players, it wasn't going to be easy spending my time outside the dressing room. When I told Coach, he smiled.

"Maybe we can figure out something," he said. "I could bring in a partition and set it up so you would still have your privacy. Would that be okay?"

"Great," I said. Anything would be better than the rest room.

I really wanted to ask Coach about the upcoming game against the Nighthawks and whether I would be able to play in it. Mom hadn't officially given her permission, but I was sure that was just a matter of time. Iggy kept telling me that I should be the number one goalie, that I was better than he was, so at least there wasn't going to be any friction on that account. Kyle came out to watch some of the practices sporting a plaster cast on his ankle. I know him fairly well and see him at school once in a while. He's a nice guy and I heard second-hand that he thought I was pretty good.

That night after practice, Mom said she wanted to talk to me. Had she made up her mind about letting me play in a game? I said a silent prayer.

"Your father and I have talked it over, and I've agreed to let you play in a game...with one provision. If you get hurt and I can see that you're not able to handle it, I'm going to insist that you only play with your brothers. At least until you're older and have grown a few inches."

"Okay," I said. I was about as excited as I've been in my whole life. I was going to be a goalie and I was about to play in a game, at least when Coach gave me the nod.

I could hardly wait.

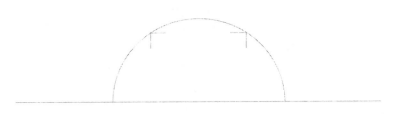

CHAPTER 6

Everybody came out to see me play against the Nighthawks, even the twins and Michael, but Coach put in Iggy. I was really disappointed but tried my best not to show it. After all, Coach hadn't said anything about me going in and Iggy was still the number one goalie on our team.

The Nighthawks scored four goals on Iggy in the first ten minutes when Coach looked over at me. "Are you ready, Katherine?" he asked. "I think it's time you got your feet wet."

"I'm ready," I said, my heart beginning to beat a little faster.

He signaled for a time out and when Iggy skated to the bench, Coach told him I was taking over. Iggy shrugged. "She should have started," he said.

As I skated toward our net, I heard a couple of comments from the Nighthawks. "Good luck, Sweetheart," one of them taunted. Another said, "Be nice to the little lady, guys."

I smiled to myself. They might be eating those words before the end of the game. I looked into the stands and could see my family all sitting in a row, my dad waving frantically and my mom sitting on her hands.

I didn't have any great expectations of us winning the game after being down by four goals, but the least I could do was not let in any more. I was hoping that Jed might score a couple and at least make it a close game. He was our leading scorer, but the Nighthawks had a rock solid defense that was hard to penetrate.

The whistle blew and I was suddenly in my first real game. I felt confident that I could keep the opposition from scoring on me, but that confidence was severely tested on their first shot. I missed it completely and by a stroke of good luck, the puck bounced off the cross bar. I guess that woke me up, because after that I managed to slam the door on the Nighthawks' attack, at least for that period.

Just before the horn blew to end the first period, Jed scored and suddenly, we were only three behind. It was only a tiny opening, but it gave our team a real lift.

Coach walked up and down in the dressing room, patting his players on the head and offering encouragement. "Katherine has given you guys a chance to win this game," he said. "If we can keep them from scoring any more goals, we've got a chance to beat them." He looked over at me. "You're doing great, Katherine. The Nighthawks are probably sitting in their dressing room right now wondering what hit them."

When we skated out onto the ice for the second period, we were a different team. We suddenly looked like winners. But the Nighthawks looked really teed off. They had had their way with Iggy, but now a little sawed off fourteen-year-old girl had shut them down for the rest of the period. That definitely didn't sit well with them and you could tell from their demeanor that they now meant business.

Our team as a whole, played much better in the second period. The Nighthawks peppered me with a lot of shots, but for the most part, I didn't have much trouble turning them back. The onslaught during our morning practices from my brothers was more fierce than what I was facing tonight.

There was no scoring in the second period and our guys definitely looked more confident as we skated into the dressing room. We were still down by 3 goals, but you never knew what could happen when a team got hot.

During the third period, I got knocked over and hit my head pretty hard on the ice. I was up almost as soon as I hit the ice, but my head hurt as well as my pride. Our team was definitely coming on and we got the better of the play during the third period, but we just couldn't make up the differential and the game ended 4 to 1.

On the one hand, I was ecstatic that I had shut out the Nighthawks, but on the other, we had lost to them again.

"You were fantastic, Kat," Jed said after the game. "You kept us in there and if we had had a little scoring punch, we might have been able to beat them."

Mom and Dad and my brothers waited for us to exit the dressing room and Mom came running up to me. "Are you all right, dear? That was an awful fall you took."

"I'm fine," I said. "It was no big deal."

"You were something else," Dad said. "Wasn't she guys?" He looked over at my brothers who were trying their best to make themselves invisible.

"She was excellent," Michael conceded. The twins nodded their heads.

"Those Nighthawks are a rough bunch," Mom said. "And they're much bigger than our team. When that big guy knocked you over, he should have gotten a penalty. Isn't there a roughing – the – goalie penalty or something?"

My dad laughed. "I think he was knocked into Kat by one of our players. But those are the breaks. Kat will have to be tough if she wants to continue playing Juvenile."

When we got home, Mom made us some hot chocolate and we all sat around talking about the game. Even the twins got their two cents worth in.

"Iggy definitely has to go," Malcolm said. "He let in too many easy ones."

"I could have stopped most of the shots he missed," John added.

"That makes it doubly important that Kat keeps playing in goal," Dad said. "If she had gone in from the beginning, you guys might have won the game."

"I still think being a goaltender is too rough for a girl," my mom joined in. "Those boys had no consideration at all for the fact that you are a girl."

"Mom, I can't play goal hoping that the opposition will take it easy on me because I'm a girl. It doesn't work like that. I have to prove that I can play just as well or better than a guy. There isn't going to be a double standard, one for me and another for the rest of the team."

"Well, there should be," my mom complained. "After all, you're smaller than they are and being a girl, you bruise easier."

"Nobody cares about that," Michael said. "If she's the goalie then she has to take what the other team dishes out, no matter what her gender."

"On that note, I think it's time we all went to bed," Dad said. "You guys have to get up early for practice. Remember?"

"How could we forget?" complained Malcolm.

I went off to my room looking forward to being by myself and thinking about the game tonight. It had gone even better than I had expected and I could scarcely wait until the next one.

The next morning, we were at it again. There was a noticeable change in my brothers though. They seemed more accepting of me. I'm not sure why. Maybe it was because I had played in a game and proved that I could play with the boys. They were still having trouble beating me, but they did score a few times on rebounds.

"When you're playing goal, it's important not to give rebounds if you can help it," Jed instructed. "Try to catch the puck or smother it, otherwise, if the shooter gets a second shot, he has a much better chance of scoring."

It was the first time Jed had given me any advice about anything, let alone goaltending. I listened and was impressed by his concern. My big brother was turning out to be a great help, something I wouldn't have believed a few months ago. Not that he was a goaltender himself, but Jed knew a lot about hockey and defense, so I paid attention.

All that week, all we did was talk hockey, hockey and more hockey. I think Mom was beginning to get weary of it. She always made sure we had done our chores and our homework. My piano practice had suffered a little, but something had to give with all the time I was spending on the ice, both at home and at practice at the arena.

The team had really accepted me, and it went without saying that I was now the number one goalie. I felt a little sorry for Iggy, but strangely, he didn't seem to mind. In fact, he was my number one cheerleader on the team, next to Coach.

We had a number of games against local teams, but they weren't the kind of competition the Nighthawks were. It was good practice and kept us sharp, but I think the whole team was anticipating our next encounter with the Nighthawks.

At school a lot of kids, mostly girls, who normally wouldn't give me the time of day, now waved at me or commented on what a great thing I was doing by playing with the boys and beating them at their own game. In our town, the girls played ringette. There was no girl's hockey team and the idea of a girl playing on a guy's team was pretty far out as far as most of the girls were concerned. A few girls obviously didn't approve, but they were in the minority.

Things went along quite nicely for several weeks until our next encounter with the Nighthawks was only a few days away. I was looking forward to it as I was certain we could beat them if I continued playing as well as I had been in the last few weeks.

It wasn't until two nights before our scheduled game when Coach paid us a visit with some bad news. The

Nighthawks were objecting to my playing on a boy's team, and would refuse to play if I was in goal. I could hardly believe my ears.

"I don't know what their beef is," Coach said. "They didn't seem to object when you played in the last game. When I talked to their coach, he said their team was against girls playing against boys. According to him they're afraid of you getting hurt."

"I can take care of myself. I already showed that I can in the last game. There must be something we can do. It isn't fair." I wanted to throw something, I was so frustrated.

"I think we're going to have to have a meeting," Dad suggested. "Get all this straightened out. There's no reason why Kat can't play if she's able."

"I'll see what I can do about setting up a meeting," Coach replied. "I'll get back to you as soon as I know something."

I could hardly concentrate at school the next day and hadn't got much sleep the night before. All my dreams seemed about to turn into a nightmare if I was kicked off the team and just when everything seemed to be coming together.

That night we all sat around waiting for the telephone to ring and give us some good news. Even my brothers thought it was unfair not to let me play.

When Coach finally did phone, he said the Nighthawks were standing firm. They wouldn't play if Katherine was in goal. "I think we should call their bluff," he said. "I have no intentions of not playing Katherine. There's no reason why she shouldn't play as far as I'm concerned."

"But what if they refuse to play?" Dad asked. "What do we do then?"

"Well, it'll be their loss. The onus will be on them to ice a team. If they refuse, then so be it. I think we have to stand firm on this and not let them push us around."

"I agree," my dad said. "So let's just see what happens."

I felt somewhat mollified. At least I wasn't going to be kicked off the team and even if they refused to play, there were other teams around who weren't concerned about a girl playing on a boy's team.

Our team took to the ice the next night and began our warm up. After several minutes and the Nighthawks hadn't made an appearance, the spectators began to chant. "We want a game, we want a game." They kept it up until the Nighthawks' coach came out of the dressing room and approached Coach. I could see the two coaches having a discussion, but tried my best to concentrate on our warm up.

The two coaches talked for several minutes, the Nighthawks coach folding his arms and shaking his head, looking as though he was standing firm on his promise of not icing his team unless I left the ice.

After about 5 minutes, the crowd again began their chant and finally their coach left and returned to their dressing room. Coach signaled to us to come over to the bench.

"He's going to talk to his team," Coach said. "If they're agreeable to play, then the game is on and they should be coming out in a few minutes. If not, I guess we won't be playing tonight. In the meantime let's just carry on with our warm up."

I skated back into the net wondering what I should do. Maybe I should just leave and let Iggy play goal. That would at least satisfy their coach until the whole matter could be resolved.

Just when I had decided to skate over and tell Coach I was willing to leave, the Nighthawks' dressing room door opened and their team skated onto the ice. I breathed a sigh of relief. I looked up into the stands and waved my stick at my mom and dad and my brothers.

Nothing more was said about my playing for our team. The game went ahead as scheduled and this time, our team scored the first goal. That seemed to set the pace for the rest of the game, as we played them evenly for three periods and ended up winning 1 to 0. I had achieved my first shutout. It was the first time we had beaten the Nighthawks in five years. But it hadn't been easy. The Nighthawks did everything in their power to score, but between our solid defense and my goaltending, we managed to keep them from scoring.

In the dressing room after the game, you'd have thought we had just won the Stanley Cup the way our team ran around high fiving, and generally acting like a bunch of wild animals. I was amazed at how important beating the Nighthawks had become. Girls wouldn't have acted this way, would they? Surely this was a guy thing.

"Nice game, Kat," Iggy said. "You were great out there."

"Thanks," I said, feeling a little strange having taken Iggy's spot away from him.

Mom and Dad and my brothers were all smiles when Jed and I came out of the dressing room.

"Here comes the next Gump Worsley," Dad teased.

"Who's Gump Worsley?" I asked.

"You don't know who Gump Worsley is?" he said. "What kind of goaltender are you?"

"He was one of the best way back when Dad was our age," Jed explained. "But you might have a ways to go before you can be compared to him."

"Well, she sure looked like him tonight," Dad insisted. "I was real proud of you, girl."

I blushed. It wasn't that often that Dad gave out compliments like that to his kids. I was touched.

"What kind of a name is Gump anyway?" I asked.

"I think it might have been a nickname. I'm not sure. But he's in the Hall of Fame. He was a real character and one of my favorite players. You know, if you're going to be a goaltender, you should read about them. You might learn something."

"I will," I promised.

"There was also Emil "The Cat" Francis," Dad added.

"Nice name," I said. "Why was he called "The Cat"?"

"Because he was so quick, like you. I guess we're going to have to call you "The Cat" now instead of just Kat."

I smiled. "Hmm, I think I like that."

As we walked to our cars, Dad took my bag and put his arm around me. "I talked to Coach after the game. He told me they played the game under protest. What a joke. Just what are they protesting? A girl played against them and shut them out. Not exactly something they'll want to draw attention to. I kind of think we've heard the last of this."

"Do you really?" I asked. "I sure hope so. I don't want to have to quit now that things are going so well."

It was so unreal. Who would have thought a few months ago, that I would be playing hockey with the Centennials and getting a shutout to boot? I could hardly believe it was happening to me. I couldn't wait to see what the rest of the year was going to bring.

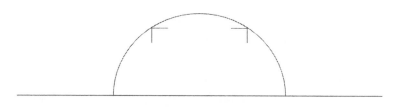

CHAPTER 7

Dad surprised us all one morning when he appeared with Ralph Jennings, the goalie for Dad's team when he had played senior hockey twenty years ago. Ralph was an outstanding goalie at the time and had agreed to come out early in the morning and help me improve my performance, something my brothers thought was pretty funny since they were already having trouble scoring on me.

Ralph was a short, stocky man with a wide grin and expressive blue eyes. According to Dad he had coached for several years after retiring from active play. He stood with Dad watching us for about ten minutes while my brothers and I went through our morning routine. I had no idea who he was at first, but just in case he was somebody important, I was doing my best to show off my skills and keep my brothers from scoring.

"Hi Katherine," he greeted me, when we took a quick break and he came striding across the ice. "I'm Ralph. I played in goal on your dad's team a long time ago. Your dad thought I might be able to give you a few tips on how to improve your goalkeeping, but I can see you don't need much help. You're a natural."

"Thank you," I replied, bursting with pride that this man who had been an outstanding goalie for years, thought I was pretty good.

"Your brothers must be proud of you."

I couldn't help but laugh at that. "Proud" wasn't quite the word I would have used. But I guess underneath all that frustration, maybe they were. Anything was possible.

Ralph proceeded to give me a few hints such as how to cut down angles, not going down too early but standing my ground and planting myself in front of the crease so the oncoming player had nothing to shoot at. I really appreciated his earnestness and at the same time his easy-going approach in explaining everything. My teachers could learn a thing or two from him.

"Two things you really need to be a good goaltender are quickness and anticipation and you've got both in spades. Also, when clearing the puck, always throw it in the corner or behind the net. Never shoot it up through the centre. It's too easy to pick off and often leads to an easy goal for the opposition. But I think one of the first things you should do is get yourself a pair of proper goalie skates. The skates you're wearing are meant for speed, not for playing goal."

I had to agree with him there, but I knew they were expensive and I didn't have the money to buy them.

After Ralph had driven away, I went over to my dad. "Thanks Dad. That was really nice of you to have Ralph come out. He was really helpful."

"You're welcome," Dad said. "He was some goalkeeper in his day I'll tell you. He kept us in a lot of games that we probably should have lost."

I guess Ralph put the bug in my dad's ear because for my fifteenth birthday, dad and mom bought me a proper pair of goalie skates. I knew they were pretty expensive, but I was very glad to get them. It took me a while to get used to them, but once I did, they were so much better than ordinary skates.

"Thank you, Dad," I told him. "I couldn't have wished for anything better."

"Nothing but the best for my little girl. You've earned them."

I think my brothers were a little upset that I got such an expensive birthday gift. My parents weren't usually very lavish when it came to gift-giving. We are a large family and money was scarce. But then again, my parents helped Jed buy his car. He was paying them back as it was more of a loan than a gift, but he might not have been able to get it without their help.

My brothers and I continued practicing every morning. Although it was only practice, I looked forward to it every day. I think I had improved quite a bit since playing with the Centennials. The twins had settled down and weren't nearly as sarcastic and whiny like they were before. They seemed to have accepted the fact that I was a good goaltender and they had to play hard to score on me.

Dad came out one morning and joined us in a little shinny game. He could skate really well and only scored on me a time or two. But to be honest, I think he was just taking it easy on me. It was really great having a dad who was so supportive and encouraging. If it hadn't been for him, I probably would never have become a goalie because he was the one who built our rink, along with the help of my brothers.

"How are the new skates?" he asked me after our practice. "Are you getting used to them?"

"I am," I answered. "It took a while, but now that I've been playing with them for a few weeks, they are much better than ordinary skates."

When I got back into the house, my mom reminded me of the recital that was coming up. "I hope you've been practicing," she said, looking over at me inquiringly.

"I'm trying," I said, "but I've been so busy, I'm probably getting a little rusty."

"Have you made up your mind what piece you're going to play?"

"I thought I would do...ah..." To be honest, I hadn't even thought about the recital and had no real idea what I wanted to play. My mind was a blank, but I knew Mom would want an answer. "I thought I might play 'Fur Elise'," I managed.

"That's a good choice, but I haven't heard you playing it lately."

"The recital isn't until Saturday. I should be able to get it ready."

She came over and sat down beside me. She had that motherly look on her face and I knew I was in for a lecture. "Hockey isn't the only thing in your life, you know. You've got your schooling and your music and your chores around here. It's wonderful having a hobby like playing hockey, but you shouldn't neglect your other duties."

"I'm trying not to," I said lamely. "It's just that hockey takes up a lot of my time and it's not like a hobby, Mom.

I'm really serious about it. I want to be really good, like the best. You know what I mean?"

Mom heaved a sigh. "You know, when I was your age, I wanted to be the best too. I wanted to be a concert pianist in the worst way. I was very good and got a lot of encouragement, but I didn't really know what I was facing. In the end, I married your dad and my dreams of being a concert pianist were lost. But I don't regret it. I've got five wonderful children and a great husband. What more could I want?"

"Oh Mom, you've never told me that. I didn't know…"

"Of course you didn't. Besides, it was only a crazy dream. I was young and romantic and your dad swept me off my feet." She laughed at the memory. "Now I've got a daughter who wants to be a goalkeeper. Who would have ever thought that?"

"I guess that seems kind of weird compared to wanting to be a pianist."

"Well, I guess it does, but if it's your dream, then why not go for it? I wouldn't want you to regret something for the rest of your life. It's too important. Your dad and I will support you all the way. But in the meantime, you've got other obligations. We're counting on you for something really special at the recital."

I swallowed. Mom organized a recital in town several times a year at the church. All twelve of her students took part. Some of them were just beginners and some were fairly accomplished and then there was me. Other students looked up to me because I had been taking lessons since I was 7 years old. I was expected to be an example for the rest of them. And here I hadn't played anything for a week, let alone practiced a piece for the recital. Anyway, I knew "Fur Elise" fairly well. It would mean just polishing it up a little. I knew I could do it. It might mean putting my goal tending on the back burner for a few days, but I guess I could sacrifice that much. And my brothers would just have to do without me for a few days. I knew what this recital meant to my mom and I didn't want to disappoint her.

As I sat backstage waiting for my turn to play "Fur Elise", I couldn't help smiling to myself. Sitting in the front row of the church was every member of the Centennials with Iggy sitting right in the middle of them right beside Coach and Jed. I could hardly believe my eyes. Who had put them up to this? It couldn't have been Mom, I was pretty sure of that or my brothers. And I didn't think Dad was this devious.

I had practiced diligently all week and had finally got my piece where I wanted it. It wasn't perfect by any means, but it was close and who would notice anyway? Nobody except my mom.

When I came out to play my piece, all the Centennials stood up and clapped. That was enough to unnerve anybody. Fortunately, I had had enough recitals behind me that an audience didn't bother me that much.

I played "Fur Elise" like I had never played it before. I don't know whether it was the occasion or because I wanted to really impress the team, but I don't mind saying, I did myself proud. When I stood up at the end and bowed to the audience, the team hooted and hollered and called my name. You would have thought that I was playing at Carnegie Hall. I was overwhelmed.

Most of the team hung around after it was all over and the people had left. Iggy was all smiles when I made an appearance. Now why hadn't I noticed what a good-looking guy he was?

"Wow! That was FAN-TAS-TIC," he said. "Right guys?"

The rest of the team, including Coach, all nodded.

"Well done, Katherine," Coach said. "You are some piano player. I'd say you're almost as good a piano player as a goalie and that's saying something."

"Thanks," I said. "Sorry about missing practice, but you can see why. I really had to bone up on this song."

Mom made an appearance. She looked very pleased and no wonder. The recital had gone off without a hitch and all the parents seemed pleased with their child's progress.

"So, Mom, what I want to know is who is responsible for this?" I pointed at the team. "I'm pretty sure they didn't just arrive spontaneously, although I would be really impressed if they had."

Mom had that knowing look about her. "I haven't the faintest idea," she said. "Why don't you ask them?"

I looked over at Iggy. If there was one member of the team that would give me a straight answer, it was Iggy. If not, I would worm it out of Jed later one way or another.

Before I could ask them, Coach said, "there were notices all over town. I merely dropped a hint that it would be nice if we came and gave you some support. And I'm sure glad we did. You were simply marvelous. Besides, these guys need a little cultural experience. Maybe some of them will even decide to take up the piano."

The team didn't look excited about that prospect.

The next night at practice, Iggy skated over to me and I knew right away that he wanted to ask me something.

Finally, he said, "how long has your mom been teaching piano lessons?"

"Why? Are you thinking of taking up the piano?" I said, giving him a big smile and wondering if he was really serious. Somehow I couldn't picture Iggy playing the piano.

He shrugged. "I might. I really enjoyed your recital and couldn't help thinking how great it would be to be able to play the piano like that."

"Well, it's hard work. I don't know how many times I wanted to quit. But my mom wouldn't let me. She said it took courage to keep doing it and not giving up like most people."

Iggy looked around at the other players and then leaned toward me. "If I took them, I wouldn't want the other guys to know, if you know what I mean."

"I don't know what you mean." I said.

"Well, I think most of the guys think...and I don't mean any disrespect here, but they most likely consider playing the piano, at least for a guy, that it's kind of..."

"Girlish," I suggested. "Not the macho thing to do?"

"Yeah. That's it. It's all right for a girl but not for a guy. Kind of dumb, eh?"

"Really dumb," I said. "A person should be proud of being able to play the piano or any other instrument for that matter and not have to hide it like he was doing something weird or freakish."

"Do you think your mom would consider taking me on as a student?"

"You're really serious, aren't you?"

He nodded. "I'm hooked. That piece you played. It was really neat. It gave me goose bumps."

I stared at Iggy for several seconds. "Did it really?" I finally said. When he nodded, I shook my head. Nobody had ever said anything like that to me. "Thanks Iggy. That was a really nice thing to say. And yes, I think my mom would love to teach you how to play the piano."

"Promise you won't tell anybody. It's important to me."

"I promise."

All during the practice, I kept thinking about Iggy and his wanting to learn to play the piano. It was so unexpected, and he seemed so keen to do it. I was quite sure that Mom, even though she already had a lot of students, would take Iggy on. He wasn't any great shakes as a goalie, but maybe he had the makings of a wonderful piano player. I hoped that I would find out.

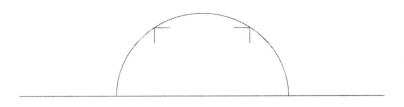

CHAPTER 8

My first year as a goalie was one of the greatest years of my life. If someone had told me at the beginning of that year that I would be in goal for the Smithville Centennials and get several shutouts, I would never have believed them. But it had happened and I was on cloud 9.

I had a lot of fun later that summer, swimming in our lake, camping and doing a lot of silly things with my girlfriends, but none of it came close to the thrill I experienced every time I skated out on the ice. I could hardly wait for the summer to be over. My brothers and I played a little street hockey with a tennis ball, but it wasn't the same. But at least it gave me a little practice and kept me sharp.

The nicest thing that had happened was that Iggy started taking piano lessons from my mom and was making exceptional progress. He didn't have a piano, so sometimes he used the one at the church and other times came out to our place and practiced on ours. It was almost like he had become a member of our family. All my brothers really liked him and Mom was impressed by how quickly he was learning the piano.

By the time freeze-up came and Dad went to work on our skating rink, I was champing at the bit to get going. The twins were equally anxious and I could see that they were more determined than ever to figure out my weakness and start filling the net with goals. But I had news for them. I had been doing a lot of reading about goaltenders and had picked up a lot of information so I was confident that I would be even better than I had been before. Bad news for my brothers.

My brother Michael would be graduating to the Juvenile ranks and would be trying out for our team. I had no doubt that he would make it. He's an excellent player, very fast and stick handles really well. It will be amazing having two brothers on the same team I'm on. I guess I wasn't going to have to worry about anyone giving me a bad time. Although my brothers had always been my tormenters, they were very loyal and wouldn't stand for anyone trying to take advantage of me.

The only thing that worried me was that Kyle's ankle was completely healed now and he was ready to resume his role as number one goaltender for the Centennials. Where did that leave me and more important, where did that leave Iggy?

I decided that I could drive myself crazy thinking about it, so I tried my best to put it out of my mind and when the first practice was called by Coach, I gathered up my equipment and went to the arena as though it was just another practice. Jed had graduated that spring and was working with my dad at the mill, but was still eligible to play so I still had a ride into practice. And having Jed on the team gave me a feeling of security. He had always been so supportive and encouraging that I knew if anything happened, he would be right there to give me a hand.

I got the shock of my life when Iggy skated out onto the ice in regular hockey gear rather than in his goalie outfit. What was going on?

"I don't think I've got much chance of making the team as a goalie," he told me, "so I'm going to try to make it as a forward."

"But you've always been a goalie," I countered.

"No I haven't," he replied. "I only went in goal a couple of years ago because there was nobody else. Before that I always played forward, left wing actually and I was pretty good too. I would much rather be a goalie to tell you the truth, but if I can make the team as a forward, that's better than nothing."

Well, I guess that solved the problem of having 3 goalies, but what if Iggy didn't make the team? How was I going to feel about that? I really liked Iggy and if I was responsible for him not making the team, I wasn't sure I could live with that.

After about ten minutes of scrimmage, I didn't have to worry any more about Iggy not making the team. He was really good. He was an excellent skater and could handle the puck as well as anybody on the team. I suddenly felt a whole lot better about things. Michael was holding his own too and looked pretty good. I had no doubt that he would make the team.

I watched Kyle a lot and realized why he had been the number one goalie. He was an excellent goaltender and not many of his team mates scored goals on him. He hadn't said much to me and I was a little worried that he would see me as a competitor rather than a teammate, but even that was resolved quite quickly toward the end of our first practice.

He skated over to me, took off his mask and gave me a big smile. "You are something else," he said. "Looks like we'll be sharing the goalkeeping duties this year."

"But you're the number one goaltender," I said. "I'm just a backup."

"Not any more you aren't. You're just as good as I am, maybe better. I'm sure Coach isn't going to be leaving you on the bench. You're too good. But don't let it worry you. I don't need to play every game. It'll be a privilege sharing duties with you."

I must have looked a little dumbfounded because he laughed and said, "Don't look so surprised. I was a little worried that I might not have a job at all. With all those shutouts you got last year, I was wondering if the Centennials were going to need me at all."

Coach played Kyle in our first game and I have to admit I was a little disappointed, but after all, Kyle was our number one goalie. Besides, the team we were playing, The Rosedale Ducks, weren't exactly the elite of the league. We beat them easily 8 to 1 and I had to admit that Kyle played well. They didn't get many shots on him, but when they did, Kyle was up to the task.

"Nice going," I said to him as he skated off the ice after the game.

He gave me a big smile. "It's your turn next and I'll bet you're going to be a lot busier than I was tonight."

Michael played in our first game and even scored a goal. I could see that Coach was impressed by his good play and the way he seemed to fit right in with the team.

Glenn **PARKER**

We were due to play the Nighthawks next week and it looked like I was going to be in goal. Interesting that Coach gave Kyle the easier game. I wondered what that was all about. I would have expected that Kyle would be starting against the stronger team. Maybe he just wanted to see how Kyle was going to stand up after being out for so long. It seemed as though his ankle had healed just fine and tonight he had proved it.

After a good week's practice, I felt confident about playing against the Nighthawks and was prepared for a real barrage. However, the Nighthawks weren't the team they had been the year before and we trounced them 6 to 1. They had lost several of their elite players who were now over aged and the young guys they had brought up from Midget weren't quite up to the task. I felt a little let down and even allowed an easy goal that I would normally have stopped. But a win was a win no matter what. It looked like we were going to be the team to beat this year.

When we returned to the dressing room, Coach informed us that there might be some changes coming about in the next few weeks. There was a big infusion of Midgets wanting to play for our team and we only had so many spots. A lot of the Midgets that didn't get chosen, and some were excellent players, would have to play in the house league and miss out on playing for the big team. A meeting was held and it was decided that since there were so many good players graduating to the Juvenile ranks that they would ice two teams.

Of course, the first thing that occurred to me was, would Kyle and I be split up and would I be playing for Coach anymore? And what about Jed and Michael? I definitely wanted to be on the same team as my brothers. I didn't ask any of those questions of course. I would just have to wait and see what happened.

"There will be a roster of each team posted on the dressing room door tomorrow night," Coach informed us. "I know some of you guys might be a little upset, but we've talked it over and decided that since we've got such a good crop of young guys coming up, they're going to need the competition if we're going to keep them in our system."

"Is this going to be a mix of our team and the new guys or is our team staying together?" one of our players asked.

"We don't want to end up with one strong team and one weaker team so we're mixing things up a bit. Some of you will be leaving our team and playing with the new team and we'll be getting some new players also," Coach informed us.

"What about the goaltenders?" Iggy wanted to know. "Are they going to be split up?"

Coach looked over at me and smiled. "Kyle and Katherine are going to be split up. I was a little worried about carrying two excellent goalies. You both deserve to be the number one stopper on your team. This way, you'll both be playing most of the games. We can't afford to have either one of you sitting on the bench half the time."

I was relieved to hear that. Sharing goal tending duties wasn't something I was thrilled about. Now it seemed, I would be the number one goalie again. But for which team?

I guess I was going to have to wait until the next night to find that out.

On the drive home, I asked Jed what he thought of the new developments.

"Makes sense to me," he replied. "There's a lot of good players this year. It would be a pity if they didn't have the opportunity we've had."

"I sure hope we're on the same team. Otherwise, how am I going to get back and forth to practice?"

"The same goes with me," Michael said. "Getting a ride into our games and practices is great and it will take some of the pressure off Mom and Dad. They must be getting tired of transporting me and the twins into practice all the time."

"I'm really hurt you guys. You're telling me that the only reason you want to be on the same team as me is that I provide a ride? And here all this time I thought, being your favorite brother, Kat, that I meant more to you than just a means of transportation."

He was doing his best to look hurt, but I knew he was kidding. "Big brother, you've been a great help and I can't thank you enough. But I still need your moral support. If we aren't on the same team, it's going to be...well, a little dicey. And I don't know whether Mom will be impressed."

"You know what? I think Coach will realize the situation and make sure all three of us are playing together. I could be wrong, but if I am, I'll put a bug in his ear."

The next day I couldn't get over to the arena fast enough to see what team I was on and whether my brothers were on my team too.

As I approached the arena, I could see a bunch of people crowded around the notice. Jed had said that he would pick me up at the arena at four o'clock after we had had a peek at what the new teams were going to look like.

As I scanned down the list of names, I could see that my brothers and I were on the same team. I breathed a sigh of relief. Good old Coach had come through in the clutch. Even Iggy was on our team. However, there were a lot of unfamiliar names and when I looked up at the top of the column, I suddenly realized that we were the new team and would have a new coach and a whole new schedule would be drawn up. I wasn't sure I liked that. I had gotten pretty used to the gang of guys that I had been playing with and I liked Coach a lot. The thought of having to get used to a new coach was a little unsettling. It wasn't everybody who had an open mind like Coach and considered a girl as a goaltender nothing to be worried about.

That night we got a call from our new coach. His name was Clarence Collins and he also was a friend of Dad's. They had played senior hockey together a long time ago. He informed me that there was going to be a meeting of the new team the next night at the arena before our first practice. At the meeting, a captain would be named and also he would take suggestions as to what the new team should be called. New uniforms would also be distributed. We were going to be sponsored by a lumber company in town so he suggested that our new name should perhaps have something to do with the lumber industry.

When I informed my brothers of the new developments, they did a high five.

"Guess we're going to be team mates, bro?" Jed said. "I hope you're ready to set me up for a record number of goals this year."

"Hey, just a minute," Michael said. "You're the one who should be feeding me and making me look good. I'm the new guy on the block."

Mom came into the room and saw us standing around looking like we had just won a prize. "What's up, kids?" she asked.

"I just got a call from our new coach," I told her. "You'll never guess who it is." When she shrugged and gave me a dubious look, I said, "Clarence Collins. What do you think of that?"

"Clarence Collins? Now there's a name I haven't heard much lately. Your dad and he were pretty friendly a long time ago. I actually went out with him a few times before I met your father."

"You did?"

"I did, and he's a very nice guy, at least he was back then. A little wild maybe, crazy is more like it, but I don't think he ever went to prison."

"Mom!"

She laughed. "I'm not exaggerating. He was a real terror at one time and a terrific hockey player as well, but other than that, he was the salt of the earth just like your father."

"Dad was never wild," I protested.

Mom gave me that Cheshire Cat smile again. "That's all I'm saying before I get myself into trouble."

My brothers and I looked at each other and shook our heads. Somehow we couldn't imagine our father as being "wild" in any way. He had always been so down to earth and hard-working and hardly ever drank. He and Mom sometimes had a glass of wine, but that was it.

"Well, I just hope he turns out to be a good coach," I said. "It doesn't matter what he was like way back when."

My mom laughed. "It wasn't THAT long ago."

Clarence Collins turned out to be six foot four and weighing about 250 pounds, most of which was definitely not muscle. He wasn't exactly handsome either. In fact, I would have called him downright homely. What had Mother ever seen in him? Well, maybe the years had simply been unkind and he looked a lot better when he was young. It was the only logical explanation.

When he walked into the dressing room and looked around at us, I think we were kind of wondering what kind of a coach he was going to be. When he spoke, I almost broke out laughing. He had this deep voice that got your attention right away. It reminded me of Paul Robeson, the guy who sang "Old Man River" in Showboat.

"Okay, listen up everybody," he said. "We've got a few things to do before we hit the ice for our first practice. First of all, we need a name for our team. Anybody got a suggestion?"

Nobody said anything for a few seconds and then Iggy put up his hand. "How about The Lumber Jacks?" he suggested.

"Sounds pretty good to me," Clarence said. "Any other names?" When nobody had any additional suggestions, Clarence said, "Well, how about we vote on it then? Everybody who would like our team name to be The Lumber Jacks put up your hand."

A number of hands went up and then slowly, as the team members looked around, more went up until almost the entire team had their hands in the air.

"It looks like we're going to be The Lumber Jacks," Clarence said. "I think since we're being sponsored by the Smithville Lumber Company, they'll be very pleased with that name. We also need to appoint a captain. Any suggestions there?"

Somebody yelled out Jed's name. Several others seconded it.

" Anybody object?" Nobody put up their hand. "Looks like you've got yourself a job, Jed. Congratulations." Jed smiled over at me.

Coach Collins pointed to several boxes by the door. "We've got new uniforms compliments of our sponsor, so go over and find one that fits you."

Several of the players went over to the boxes and began sorting through the uniforms. I was looking at Iggy. He was busy putting on his goaltending gear. "I thought you were going to play forward," I said.

Iggy grinned. "I'd much rather play in goal. I've always liked it better."

I wanted to tell him that he might not be playing in many games, but he seemed to read my mind and said, "I don't mind being the backup. The team needs two goalies and I'll get all the practice I'll need during our scrimmages. Anyway, maybe I'll get into some of the games — when we play a weaker team. What do you think?"

"I think you're right. And I think you don't give yourself enough credit. You're a very good goalie."

"Well, I try, but I've got a ways to go to catch you."

I walked over to the boxes and grabbed a uniform. They were a gaudy red and yellow with Smithville Lumber Co. emblazoned on the back. It seemed awfully big when I tried it on, but I wasn't wearing any of my equipment so it would probably do.

When everyone had a uniform, Coach Collins again stood in the middle of the room. "I think most of you guys..." He glanced over at me "and Katherine there, know me or know of me. I've been out of the loop for a little while, but I still have a real passion for hockey. I'm too fat to play anymore so the next best thing is to coach."

There was a smattering of laughter amongst the players. I wondered where he had been while he had been "out of the loop". In prison?

"I expect a hundred percent from you guys if you want to stay on the team. I also expect you to do your utmost to protect our little goaltender there. It's not every team that's got a girl goaltender, and if any of our competition tries to take advantage of her size, I expect you guys to step up to the plate. Any questions about that?" He glared at us.

No one said anything and a few of the new players glanced over at me.

I think my face must have gone red. I hadn't expected to be singled out like that. I did my best to look unconcerned.

"Okay, tonight we're just going to do some wind sprints, a few line rushes and end with a short scrimmage. I'll see you all out on the ice." With that, he left the room. Everybody looked around not sure what to say.

"I don't think I want to get on his bad side," someone chirped. "Man, is he big!"

"A regular Paul Bunyan," someone else added. Everybody laughed.

I pulled my partition over from the corner and started changing into my gear. Clarence was so unlike Coach, I wondered if I was in for a long year. I had gotten so used to Coach's laid back way of coaching that anything more rigorous was going to be a challenge. And I wasn't sure I wanted extra protection from my teammates. I wanted to be treated like any other goalie.

When we got home that night, Mom and Dad were in the kitchen having something to eat. I could see they were dying to find out all about our new coach. The twins came bounding downstairs, almost as keen to hear about our news as Mom was.

"Jed got named captain," I said.

"Good for you." Mom smiled proudly over at Jed. "So? What's he like? Your coach I mean. Did you like him?"

"He's awfully big," Michael said.

"And he's got a very deep voice," Jed said.

"And he's kind of..." I wanted to say intimidating or scary or something, but I didn't want my parents worrying. "Kind of strict." It was the only word I could think of.

"You don't like him," Mom said.

"It's too early to tell," Jed said. "I thought our first practice went pretty good. He seems to know his hockey well enough."

"He ought to," Dad said. "I taught him everything he knows."

"Oh Dad," I said. "Be serious."

"I am serious. He's a couple of years younger than me. I took him under my wing when he first joined our team. He was pretty wet behind the ears."

"I'll bet he's doesn't like having a girlie on his team," Malcolm said.

"Yeah," John agreed. "What did he say about that?"

I smiled at the twins. "Nothing, absolutely nothing. He just wanted to know if it was true that I had twin brothers who couldn't score on me. I told him it was, and he said you could give him a call and he would give you a few pointers."

"Oh sure," Malcolm said. "We believe you."

The twins didn't have much to say after that.

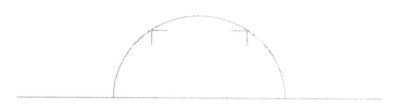

CHAPTER 9

Our first game was going to be against my old team, The Centennials. It became quite obvious that Coach Clarence was anxious to win his debut coaching game, so he really put us through some strenuous practices to get ready for it.

I was excited about playing my old team. I was thinking that the result might come down to who performed the best, Kyle or me. We were a new team with a lot of young players, but what we lacked in experience, we made up for with speed and enthusiasm. The Centennials were more experienced and bigger than we were, and were probably just as eager to win their first game as we were.

I made some key saves in the first period that kept us in the game. The Centennials came out of the gate fast and had us running around and looking a little befuddled. It wasn't until almost the half way mark of the first period that we got our first shot on goal. Kyle had no problem stopping it. When we tromped into the dressing room at the end of the first period, we were breathing a sigh of relief that the score was still tied 0-0. We had been thoroughly outplayed and we knew it.

Coach Collins gave us a little pep talk and some sound advice about what to do when we didn't have the puck and seemed to be running around aimlessly.

"Don't panic whatever you do," he said. "And get off the ice when you're tired. I don't want anybody staying out there for more than a minute."

The second period was much more even, but we were still outplayed. I had a number of really tough saves and my friend the crossbar came through a few times. Jed had several good shots at Kyle and even Michael got in a shot or two, but Kyle was equal to the task. It looked like this was going to be a scoreless tie.

In the third period at about the 12 minute mark, Jed got a breakaway, deked Kyle on the left side and threw the puck up over the goaltender's pads. We were actually ahead 1 to 0. I could see my parents standing up and cheering, waving their arms and yelling encouragement. It gave me a warm feeling to think how supportive my parents were. It wasn't every parent who would spend a weeknight in a cold arena watching a hockey game when they could be doing something far more interesting.

The Centennials went on a blitz and came at us with everything they had, but we held them off and skated into the dressing room with our first win as the Lumberjacks. Coach Clarence was beside himself with delight.

"You guys did yourselves proud tonight," he said. "I think you should all be taking Katherine out for dinner the way she played. She saved our bacon in the first period especially. Nice going Katherine."

When I got home Mom and Dad treated us like we had just won the Stanley Cup. Dad especially was very excited and said he hadn't enjoyed a hockey game like that for a long time.

"By gosh, I sure must have taught that Clarence a thing or two," he said. "After that first period, you guys really settled down and played some pretty sound hockey. What did old Clarence say to you during the intermission anyway?"

In a very deep voice, Jed imitated Coach Clarence perfectly. "He told us to hang in there, don't panic and stay cool. Words of wisdom don't you think?"

"How about that shutout?" Mom said. "You were terrific dear. But my heart was in my mouth at some of those slap shots they took. Aren't you afraid you'll get hurt?"

"Oh Mom, you get used to that. Besides, most of them missed the net and a couple of them the crossbar took care of. But it was great getting a shutout in my first game with the new team."

"And it won't be the last one," Jed intoned. "From now on we'll be expecting a shutout in every game. Right Michael?"

Michael shrugged. "I guess." He didn't look half as enthusiastic about our game as my parents or Jed. And then it occurred to me that nobody was paying any attention to his debut as a Juvenile. No wonder he was looking a little glum.

"You played a really strong game, Michael. And you had some good shots on goal. You were just unlucky that one of them didn't go in," I told him.

He managed a smile. "Thanks," he said, looking at my parents, who came over and gave him a hug.

"We haven't forgotten you," Mom said. "You were perfect in your first game. I was so proud. Some people beside us were asking who you were and I told them you were my son and that was your very first game as a Juvenile and with both your brother and your sister. They were very impressed."

Michael's smile was at first tentative and then grew into a full fledged beam. Wasn't it wonderful, I thought, what a few kind words could do? I vowed not to forget to compliment Michael on his next game.

We all retired in a good mood. I could scarcely wait for morning to inform the twins who were sleeping over at a friend's place that night about my shutout. Somehow I didn't think it was going to make their day.

Later that week I got a call from a reporter who worked for the local newspaper, The Smithville Chronicle. He told me his name was Brian Carson and he wanted to do an article about me for the newspaper. He said that being a girl playing for a boy's team and getting a shutout was big news and he was wondering if we could meet somewhere.

I was a little taken aback but at the same time also a little flattered that a reporter actually wanted to write about me. "Sure," I said. "I could meet with you. As long as my brother is with me. Could we meet in a restaurant maybe? It would have to be after school too."

"That would be great. How about Herby's on Main Street? I could meet you anytime this week after three-thirty. I'll even spring for a coke or whatever you want to eat."

"I'm busy tomorrow, but how about Thursday at about quarter to four?"

"Thursday it is," he said. "I'll look forward to it."

When I told Jed, he couldn't help smiling. "Hmm. Looks like your fame is spreading far and wide. Should be interesting to see what kind of questions he asks. Don't tell anybody about it though. We'll just let it be a surprise when the story appears in the paper."

During the next few days, I found it hard to keep from spilling the beans. Of course, I told Tracy and she swore not to tell anybody. She was just as excited as I was.

"Gee, if you keep this up, you won't even want to talk to the likes of me. You'll be too famous."

I knew she was only kidding, but I put my arm around her and said, "You'll always be my best friend, Trace, no matter what happens."

When Jed and I got to Herby's Restaurant, we were a little early so we found a booth as far away from the other patrons as we could. I had no idea what Brian Carson looked like, so we kept our eyes on the entrance hoping to see someone who looked like he might be a reporter.

Five minutes after we arrived, Brian Carson made his entrance, looked around, saw us sitting in the far corner and walked over to us. He was tall and gangly but had a friendly face and an open manner.

"Hi, I'm Brian," he said, sliding in across from us. He held out his hand and we both shook it. "Nice to meet you. And congratulations on that shutout the other night, Katherine."

"Thanks," I said.

"As I mentioned on the phone," he went on, "I would like to do a little article on you if you don't mind answering a few questions."

"Fire away," I said, glancing over at Jed who was sitting back looking as though he was going to enjoy this.

"First of all, what would you like to drink? It's on me."

Jed and I both ordered cokes and Brian a coffee. It took several minutes for our drinks to arrive and in the meantime, Brian did his best to break the ice and try to make Jed and me feel relaxed. He seemed like a genuinely nice guy and he made me laugh a few times with a couple of good anecdotes about hockey players.

Finally, he asked me a whole lot of questions including what made me want to become a goalie, what was it like playing on a boy's team, who was my inspiration and did I intend to continue playing after high school. He also wanted to know what my parents thought of it. I tried to answer his questions as honestly as I could. Jed chipped in a few times when I was at a loss as to how to answer a question. Brian made copious notes as we went along.

"My dad calls me "The Cat" all the time," I added. "After Emile "The Cat" Francis who played for the New York Rangers a long time ago, back in the 1950's. He was kind of one of my dad's heroes."

"A very appropo name," Brian said. "I like it."

"My dad played for the senior team here for several years. Maybe you've heard of him. Frank Rollins?"

"Of course. I should have made the connection. He was some player all right. Seems like you got good genes."

I glanced over at Jed. He looked about as pleased as I've ever seen him.

When we had finished, Brian held out his hand and we shook it again. "That was great. I think I've got everything I wanted to know. I'll be writing the article in the next few days, but I can't honestly tell you when it will be published. Hopefully within a week or two." He pulled out a camera from his backpack and put it on the table. "I almost forgot. I'd like to get a photo of you if you don't mind."

I shrugged. "I guess I don't mind, if you aren't afraid of your camera breaking."

He smiled at my attempt at humor, picked up his camera and snapped a picture of me. "Haven't broken one yet. But to be honest, I think my camera is safe. It isn't every day that I get to take a photo of a female goaltender and a pretty one at that."

Brian Carson had definitely won me over with that comment, even though I blushed and almost uttered, "aw shucks".

"What did you think of him?" I asked Jed on our way home.

"He seemed like a nice enough guy. I guess we'll find out when the article comes out. It'll be a nice scrapbook item for you to show your grandkids when you're old and gray and famous."

"Famous? I hardly think so, but I'm having the time of my life right now. It's so much fun playing against the guys and actually succeeding at it. Wow! I can't wait to see what he says in the article. I've never had anybody write about me before."

"Get used to it. The way you're playing, there might be a lot more newspaper articles to come."

"Do you really think so?"

"Of course. You're not only a goaltender, but a girl goaltender who's getting shutouts against the guys. Now if that ain't news, I don't know what is."

Jed's comment made me even more excited about the upcoming article in the newspaper.

The article didn't appear until the next week and was on the front page of the newspaper instead of the sports page. Jed was the first to get a copy and brought it home for me to read. Mom and Dad and the rest of my brothers didn't know anything about the article, so I was hoping it would be a pleasant surprise.

The photo of me made me laugh when I saw it accompanying the article. I had the look of a deer trapped in headlights and my mouth was open as though I was about to swallow something. Not my most flattering photograph.

The article was entitled LOCAL MISS SHUTS OUT FORMER TEAMMATES by Brian Carson

> *Katherine Rollins, better known as "The Cat", to her family, made her debut as the goaltender with the Smithville Lumberjacks and shut out her old team The Centennials in an exhibition that could only be termed "phenomenal" according to her coach, Clarence Collins.*

> *Katherine, 15, is a grade 10 student at James Wilson High School and the daughter of Frank Rollins, the one time high scoring center for the now defunct Smithville Rockets.*

> *"She is definitely one of the finest prospects we've had in Smithville for a long time," Collins said. "She plays goal like a veteran and no one would suspect that she was a girl until she takes her mask off and flashes that captivating smile."*

When I asked Katherine how a young girl managed to become a goaltender, she seemed reluctant to answer the question. Her brother, Jed Rollins, who plays on the same team, informed me that it was a bribe that went wrong. But once Katherine got a taste of beating her brothers, she was hooked.

"It's hard to explain," she said. "But I really enjoy it, I guess because I'm good at it and it gives me a lot of satisfaction to be able to compete with the guys."

Compete with the guys she does! From what I've been able to learn, she practically shuts the door on her teammates at practice and does it with the grace of a....cat.

Katherine has four brothers, all hockey players, and they play every morning on their home-made rink. Michael, 16, plays with the Lumberjacks as well, making it a true family affair.

As to what Katherine hopes to achieve as a goaltender in the future, she replied that she hopes to make lots more shutouts. We think she'll be successful in that endeavor and wish her the best.

After Jed finished reading it to me, he glanced up. "Well, what do you think?"

"It's awesome," I said. "I mean, I really like it. Do you?"

"It's pretty complimentary. Couldn't have done a better job myself. Now that photo could use a little touching up. You look a little like you've been caught with your hand in the cookie jar."

"I didn't have a chance to strike a pose," I said. "He kind of caught me off guard. But I suppose I'm recognizable. I should have worn something a little more feminine. The last thing I want is to be considered a tomboy. And no, I don't think the fashion magazines will be calling any time soon."

When Mom and Dad got home, we showed them the article and they were thrilled.

"My," Mom said, "I never dreamed any of my children would end up being a celebrity."

Mom could be a great tease at times, but I could see she was really pleased. Her previous worries about me getting hurt seemed to have disappeared and I was relieved about that. I didn't want my mom worrying about me.

When the twins and Michael read the article, there was a mixed response. The twins were typically indifferent, but Michael was pleased, especially seeing his name in it. It seems I had won over two of my brothers. It was just a matter of time before the twins came around. I was sure of it. They were still chaffing about not being able to score on me, but now that I had a shutout, maybe they wouldn't think it was such a big deal.

Iggy came over that night to practice the piano and gave me a hug after reading the article. The only people who hugged me were my parents and they didn't do it that often. It felt good to have such a great friend like Iggy, who wasn't afraid to express his feelings in a physical way.

Mom had suggested that Iggy and I learn a duet to play at the recital that was coming up again. Iggy had made such strides in his music, that I didn't have any doubts that we could play a duet together and pull it off. It was just a matter of finding an appropriate piece.

"Any ideas?" I asked him.

He began going through his books, looking for a piece that he felt confident enough to play in front of an audience. "How about 'Nocturne by Chopin?"

"Excellent choice," I said. "When do you want to start practicing?"

"No time like the present," he said, going over to the piano and sitting down.

I went over and sat beside him. It seemed strange sitting beside someone at the piano. I had never played a duet with anybody except my mom and even with her it wasn't something we did very often. This was going to be a challenge.

"So? Do you know Nocturne?" I asked, flipping through our sheet music to find it.

"Sort of," Iggy said. "But not very well. Maybe you can give me a few tips on how to play it."

For the next hour, Iggy and I worked on "Nocturne" and by the end of the hour, we were playing it as though we had been playing together all our lives. Mom was in the kitchen listening and when we finished practicing, she came in and congratulated us.

"That was really good you two. And only one practice. I'm impressed. By the time the recital rolls around you guys will be right on top of things."

Iggy was clearly pleased and grinned over at me. It was amazing how Iggy had adopted our family and how we had adopted him. He clearly enjoyed our company and came over ever more frequently. We were always glad to see his smiling face.

From what I could learn from Iggy, his parents, although quite well off and able to give him everything he wanted, didn't have a lot of time for Iggy and I suspected because of that, he was quite lonely. Being an only child was one thing, but having parents who were distant and unavailable must have been hard on him.

"You're welcome to come over any time," my mother always said to him, and she meant it. He often ate with us and spent most of the evening with us playing games or just talking. When we had hockey practice or a game, neither of his parents ever showed up to watch him play. That in itself must have hurt him deeply.

My brothers and I continued our morning practices. I always looked forward to them, especially now that both Michael and Jed were on my team. When we practiced in the arena, I didn't see much of my brothers. I was too busy stopping pucks to even notice who was shooting at me, and they were concentrating on their own games and trying to get better.

The twins were definitely improving and getting bigger it seemed, by the day. They would be in their last year of Midget. Jed would be too old, but eventually there could be 4 players from the Rollins family playing together. The thought of playing on the same team as the twins amused me. In their present frame of mind, I don't think the prospect would appeal to them very much, but it was still a year away. Who knew how they would feel in a year.

The scrimmages in our back yard became more and more animated as the winter continued. The twins, in their eagerness to prove themselves, tried everything in their power to score points, whether it was a body check, a head high slap shot or just a lot of needling against both their brothers and me. In a way, I felt sorry for them. They really were excellent players, excellent skaters and stick handlers, but they still thought of themselves as being not as good as the rest of us and somehow outcasts. That chip on their shoulders had to come off sometime and as far as I was concerned, the sooner the better.

Our next game was against the Nighthawks. We hadn't seen much of them this year, but it was rumored that they had imported a few players to shore up their defense and give them some scoring punch from the blue line.

On the night of our game, Mom and Dad were again sitting in the stands. With three of their kids playing for the Lumberjacks, there was no way they were going to miss a game. Besides, I think Mom wanted to keep an eye on me like a mother hen looking after her chick.

For some reason, the game was rough, even chippy at times, and the referee called a lot of penalties. That meant there were a lot of power plays on both sides that put extra pressure on me. I was used to about 25 shots a game, but in this game, I had to handle almost twice that many. I didn't mind being busy, but when we were short handed, I was that much more vulnerable to their attack. And that was why I didn't get a shutout that night. I let in two goals, one I was screened on completely and the other I was flat on my back. However, we still managed to squeak out a victory, 3 to 2.

Coach Collins was about as happy as I've ever seen a human being, grinning from ear to ear, and not able to say enough good things about our team.

"You guys were great," he told us. "They might be bigger and more fierce, but you guys are faster and smarter. I was so proud. And seeing you executing some of the things we've been practicing, that was the most gratifying thing of all. It means you guys are paying attention and doing what you need to do to win. That's what I call team work."

I was hoping that Iggy would get into the game if we got up a bunch of goals, but as it turned out, the game was too close and Iggy sat on the bench the whole game. I still couldn't help feeling badly about that. I knew Iggy wanted to get into some of the games and I was hoping that would happen soon. Nobody wanted to sit on the bench while the rest of the team got to play.

Iggy always complimented me on my game and never seemed to mind not playing himself, but I knew that would only last for so long before he lost interest and dropped out and I didn't want that to happen.

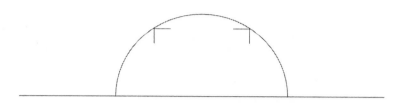

CHAPTER 10

The winter of 1982 turned out to be one of the best winters I've ever spent, especially since our team, The Lumberjacks, did so well in the league. And I knew that I had been a pivotal part of that success. We only lost a couple of games by close scores and I was happy to sit out a few times so that Iggy could get a few games under his belt. In the games he played, we won and won big. It gave me a chance to see our team from a different perspective and also gave Iggy an opportunity to show what he could do. As it turned out, he did really well. I think he surprised even himself at how good he was.

Although I had doubts about Coach Collins at the beginning of the year, he turned out to be one fabulous coach. Not only was he encouraging and supportive, but always seemed to be able to criticize and offer suggestions without hurting anyone's feelings.

Jed and Michael also had a good year with the team, and ended up being number one and two in scoring. This was to be Jed's last year of Juvenile and when I asked him what he planned to do the next year, he told me he was going to attend the training camp of one of the Junior B teams, the Lakeland Hornets. They were holding a camp for newcomers during August in Lakeland, which was over 200 hundred miles away from our place.

Of course, I was intensely curious about the team and asked Jed if I could come and have a look at what kind of team the Hornets were and what their goalies were like. Jed had no objections, but he said he couldn't bring me back home because he was staying there for at least a week, maybe more, so I would have to find my own way back. In the end, Iggy volunteered to take me and bring me home. It would also give him a chance to see how good the goalies in Junior B were compared to Juvenile goalies.

I had turned 16 during the winter and gained some height and weight. I had begun lifting weights and doing calisthenics to get stronger. If I was going to be competing with the guys, I had to show them that I was just as strong and capable as they were. Of course, I didn't want to end up being too muscular, what girl of 16 does, but I wanted to be in good shape and well toned for the ever-demanding role as a number one goaltender. Little did I know what that consisted of.

The winter of 1982 became memorable for another reason. Iggy and I played a duet at Mom's recital and it was the toast of the town. Believe it or not, Brian Carson heard about it and was right there in the front row applauding and yelling bravo with the best of them. Of course, he wanted a story and after the recital was over, he came backstage and interviewed us, took our picture and wrote an article in the next Chronicle. Iggy was thrilled, of course. Nobody had ever paid him much mind, least of all his parents, so having an article in the paper about him was pretty special. I think he might have even got his parents' attention.

Iggy and I began spending a lot of time together. At first we were just good friends and team mates, but as the winter progressed and turned into spring, we began to look at each other in a different way. And when Iggy invited me to his prom, I knew he liked me a lot. I didn't find it difficult to accept Iggy as a boyfriend as opposed to just a friend. I think Mom was a little worried about that. I was too young, she said. But Iggy is such a nice guy and so open and transparent, that I think she realized that there wasn't much to worry about.

The twins were slowly beginning to grow up a bit. They weren't nearly as sarcastic and hard to get along with as they had been previously. I think Iggy had something to do with that. They both liked him a lot and seeing that we were an item now, the twins seemed to respect that and acted accordingly.

We had a great time over the summer holidays. I tried my best to stay in shape for the next winter's hockey season. It was a lot easier to do with Iggy exercising right along with me. We went on some long drives on weekends and had several picnics and we swam in our lake almost every day. I worked several nights a week at the local theater selling tickets and dispensing popcorn. I didn't make a lot of money, but it was nice having a few dollars of my own without depending on Mom and Dad for spending money. My music suffered and so did Iggy's, but we knew that come Fall, we would get back into our routine of practicing the piano and maybe even playing another duet together.

All summer I looked forward to going to Lakeland to see Jed's tryout and also to watch their goalies. It was going to be fascinating to see how good they were and whether I would ever be good enough to play for them.

On a hot morning in mid-August, Jed in his Volkswagen and Iggy driving his Toyota with me in the front seat beside him, drove out of our yard and headed for Lakeland. To say I was excited would be an understatement. I was exhilarated.

I promised Mom and Dad that we would be back that night which meant a lot of driving, but we figured we could do it without too much trouble. The camp started at noon and lasted until 4 o'clock. If we were on the road shortly after 5, we should be able to get home before 10.

When we arrived at the arena, we could see lots of other players going in the entrance with their equipment bags over their shoulders and carrying several sticks. Jed had only talked to the coach over the telephone, but it didn't take long to zero in on him once we were inside. He was sitting at a desk they had temporarily set up with a questionnaire sheet and an application form. His name was George Sinclair and he looked about the same age as Dad.

"This is my sister, Katherine," Jed told him. "And her friend Iggy. Katherine is an outstanding goalie and played for our team last winter. She had several shutouts. Iggy is a goaltender as well and is our backup."

Coach Sinclair seemed immediately interested. "Good goaltenders are as rare as hen's teeth around here," he said. "And a wee girl at that. Hmm." He looked thoughtfully at me and then at Iggy. "Are you here for a tryout?" he wanted to know.

"Oh, no," I said. "We're just here to watch Jed and size up your goaltending prospects."

"Too bad," he said. "We've only got one goaltender coming and we could sure use another, maybe even two. Sure you don't want to gear up and give it a try?"

"I'd love to," I said immediately, "but I...we didn't bring our gear."

"Well, that's one thing you wouldn't have to worry about. We got more goalie equipment in our dressing room than we'll ever use. I'm sure you could find some that would suit you. Now skates might be a problem, but we might be able to find a pair to fit you. Skates for Iggy wouldn't be a problem."

Was he serious? I wondered. I looked over at Iggy, who had a big smile on his face. "Sounds like fun, doesn't it? What do you think?"

"Why not, Kat? What have you got to lose?"

"Did you mean just for this afternoon or for the whole week?" I asked Coach Sinclair.

"Depends on how you do. I might be making some cuts after the first look-see. If you aren't what we're looking for, it would be just for today."

"I don't think you're going to be disappointed," Jed informed him. "Kat might be a girl, but she's one heck of a goalie."

"I'll second that," Iggy said.

"But where would we stay?" I asked. "And I didn't bring any clothes."

"Let's not get ahead of ourselves," Coach Sinclair said. "We can deal with that eventuality if we like what we see. Until then, just try your best and we'll see what happens."

My head was in a whirl. Iggy and I had come here to be spectators and now it looked like we were going to get a tryout. Holy catfish! What an opportunity. I could hardly believe this was happening.

"What do you think, Iggy? Should we do it?"

"Does a rabbit live in the forest? Of course we should do it? I think it would be a blast."

Of course I hadn't even thought about what we would do if we made the team. It would mean leaving home and living in Lakeland. I wasn't sure I was prepared to do that. And would Mom and Dad even allow such a thing? They still considered me a child, even though I was sixteen and would be almost seventeen when the hockey season rolled around.

It didn't take us long to find enough equipment. There was a lot of it strewn around the equipment room in the player's dressing room. Iggy was able to find a pair of skates that fit him, but I was having difficulty finding any my size. Coach Sinclair finally got on the phone and talked to his daughters who both had skates and were willing to bring them to the arena. Within 10 minutes, I had two pairs of skates to try on and luckily, one pair fit fairly well. I wasn't going to be as steady on my feet as I would have been in my own skates, but they would do. I had to dress in the visitor's dressing room as the main dressing room was filled with young male hopefuls who, I'm sure, wouldn't have appreciated having a 16-year-old girl watching them get dressed. Not to mention my own privacy.

When Iggy and I skated onto the ice, it felt totally unreal. Players wheeled around us as they warmed up, banging their sticks on the ice and passing a puck back and forth. We went up to the other goalie and introduced ourselves. His name was Kirk Andrews and he had just graduated from Juvenile just like Jed. He didn't look much more than 16, but told us he was 18.

We began skating around the ice, trying our best to warm up and get used to different skates. Iggy looked so relaxed and easy-going, I envied him. I felt a little out of place. Would these guys accept me as readily as my team at home? What would they think of a girl playing on a guy's team? I guess the only thing I could do to convince them of that was to play well, and keep them from scoring. But I could see right away that these players were bigger, stronger and better skaters than the guys on our team. And they could make harder shots than any I had faced before. I hoped I hadn't bitten off more than I could chew.

My first test came about 5 minutes later. Coach Sinclair had his hopefuls line up along the blue line and take shots at us. At first it wasn't very difficult. I think the players thought that because I was a girl, they should take it easy on me. However, when I managed to stop everything they threw at me, they began to shoot in earnest. I really didn't mind handling slap shots traveling 100 miles an hour, as long as they kept them below shoulder height, but wearing unfamiliar equipment made me feel a little sluggish and a few of them got by me. But for the most part, I think I handled myself quite well.

Later, during a scrimmage, I was the only goalie who didn't get scored on. I felt pretty good about that. Coach Sinclair approached me as we went off the ice for a brief intermission and pep talk.

"Holy Hanna, girl, where did you learn to play goal like that?"

"In our back yard mostly," I replied. "I've got four brothers and they keep me busy. They all shoot pretty hard."

Coach Sinclair scratched his head. "In all my years of coaching, I haven't seen anything like what you just did out there. That was some performance. How old did you say you were?"

"Sixteen," I said. "But I'll be seventeen in December."

"Who's been coaching you?"

"I learned mostly on my own," I said, "but I've got a couple of books and Ralph Jennings gave me a few tips. He used to be the goalkeeper for the Smithville Rockets."

"The fans in Lakeland are going to LOVE you girl. In fact, they'll probably go a little off the deep end if you keep making saves like you just did. They've never seen a girl goalkeeper before. You're going to be a sensation."

I didn't know quite how to respond to Coach Sinclair's enthusiasm. Did it mean he wanted me to play for his team? But how could I do that? I lived in Smithville. That was over 4 hours from here.

During our intermission Coach Sinclair talked to the players, told them what to expect if they made his team. Not many of them would make it if that was the best they could do. They had to give one hundred percent every second they were on the ice, otherwise they were wasting their time.

"And I expect you guys to be able to put a few pucks past Katherine here. She's awfully good as you no doubt have already discovered, but guys, she's a girl and she's only sixteen. Get with the program."

I didn't like that little speech at all. What was the coach trying to do anyway? I didn't want all these guys mad at me, blaming me if they didn't make the team. I was just trying to do my best like the rest of them. I could see that Jed was streaks ahead of most of them. I didn't think Jed was going to have any trouble making the team. As for Iggy, I wasn't sure. He was still smiling but that was no measure of how he was doing because Iggy smiled all the time.

Back on the ice, Coach Sinclair put the young hopefuls through their paces with wind sprints and stops and starts until most of them could barely stand up on their skates. I did my best to keep up, but I knew I wasn't in the greatest of shape. I was beginning to regret that I hadn't taken my training more seriously during the summer.

After the practice, Coach Sinclair, a grin as wide as the Mississippi, came over and shook my hand. "That was a great performance out there this afternoon little lady. You aren't planning on running off on me now, are you? You've got my official invitation for the rest of the camp."

I shook my head and looked over at Iggy. "My parents are expecting us back tonight."

Coach Sinclair looked panic stricken. "How about coming into my office and talking about this?" he said, leading us over to a small room just off the mezzanine area. He flicked on some lights, sat down on an easy chair and gestured for us to have a seat opposite him.

"Now, what's the urgency about getting home? Parents worried about you?"

"They always worry about me," I replied. "But we did tell them we would be back around 10 o'clock tonight. We hadn't expected to take part in the camp. We came to see Jed mostly."

"Well, I would sure appreciate it if you could stick around. We can sure use you, both of you actually. Fact is, you looked good enough out there that you might have a chance of being either our backup or our number one goalie. Sound interesting to you?"

Both Jed and Iggy were smiling over at me. This was crazy, I thought. Staying for the camp was a dream come true, but...what would Mom and Dad think? And where would I stay?

"I'd love to stay and I think Iggy would too, but I don't think my parents would allow it."

"Leave your parents to me," George said. "I'll talk to them. What's your phone number?"

I gave him our phone number and sat looking out the window as Coach Sinclair dialed the number. I didn't trust myself to look at Iggy and Jed. Were they as keen about this as I was? Jed was staying anyway, but how did Iggy feel about it? I was dying to ask him.

"Hello, is this Mrs. Rollins? My name's George Sinclair. I'm the coach of the Lakeland Hornets and your daughter Katherine is here along with your son Jed and Iggy. I invited them to our tryout camp and Katherine really impressed us."

I could hear Mom saying something but couldn't make out what it was.

"All three of them are here right now with me. What I want to know is, would it be all right if Katherine stayed with the camp for a week? We'll find accommodation for her. She won't have to worry about that. In fact, she can stay at our house. We got lots of room and plenty of things to keep her busy."

There was a long pause before Mom spoke. I could just visualize her rolling her eyes and wondering what her wayward daughter was up to now.

"Mrs. Rollins, Katherine really wants to do this." He glanced over at me and winked. "She's a great girl and we'll make sure she's well taken care of. I've got two girls just about her age. They'll have a ball together. And don't worry about clothes. My daughters have more clothes than they'll ever use."

There again was a long pause, and then Mom said something. "She's right here in front of me. Do you want to talk to her?" He then handed me the phone.

"Hi Mom," I managed. "Would it be okay if I stay. I think everything will be fine. And Jed's here. He'll look after me."

"Katherine, what is going on? I thought you were just going over to watch Jed practice. Now you're trying out for their team?"

"I am. I didn't intend to, but they were short a goalie or two so they invited Iggy and me to try out. And we've been doing really well."

"But all your equipment is here and your skates."

"Coach Sinclair was able to find all the equipment we needed so that was no problem."

"I'll talk it over with your dad," Mom said. "Phone me in about an hour. But don't get your hopes up too high. I'm not sure I like what's going on." With that, she hung up.

Jed looked at me expectantly. "So what did she say? Is it a go?"

"She's going to talk to Dad. I have to get back to her."

Coach Sinclair was all smiles. "If I know anything about human nature, your mom will come through. And just in case she doesn't," he added with a twinkle in his eye, "we'll just have to go to Plan B."

"And what's that?" I asked.

"Just you leave that to me," he said. "I've had a lot of dealings with parents so I'm very experienced in that area."

We went over to Coach Sinclair's house and I met his daughters. Silvia, his oldest, was just my age. In fact our birthdays were only a few days apart. Sandra was a few years younger. They both seemed like nice girls and were excited that I might be staying with them for the rest of the week. They had a spare bedroom that I could use and Silvia was able to find lots of clothes for me to wear. They were a little large for me as Silvia was a few inches taller than me, but they would do.

When the hour was up, I phoned back and Dad answered this time. "How's my favorite goalie?" he asked. "Are you keeping all those junior hockey players at bay?"

"Hi Dad," I said. "Iggy and I are having a great time and Coach Sinclair is really nice. He wants us to stay for the entire camp. Do you think it would be O.K.?"

"Well, I don't think your mom's too happy about it, but we talked it over and if you're sure about this, I guess it'll be all right."

"Thanks Dad. I'll tell you all about it when we get home."

Jed, Iggy and Coach Sinclair were all smiles when I hung up. "Sounds like a go," Jed said.

I nodded. "Mom's not that keen, but I guess Dad talked her into it." I looked over at Coach Sinclair. "Thanks for everything. Are you sure I won't be a nuisance?"

"You just make yourself at home," he said. "My daughters are tickled pink that you're here. It isn't often they get to hobnob with a girl goaltender."

Once I got settled into my new bedroom, there was a knock on the door and Silvia appeared. "Can I come in?" she asked.

"Of course," I said.

She came in and sat in a chair across from me. "It's really neat having you stay," she said. "I've got a million questions for you."

"Like what?" I asked.

"Like why do you want to be a goalie? How did you get so good at it? Aren't you afraid of getting hurt? What are the boys like on your team? Questions like that."

I had to laugh. Silvia was so earnest and looked genuinely concerned. She was a lot like Tracy – very feminine and ladylike. But I really liked her. I tried my best to answer her questions, but I'm not sure she was entirely convinced. But I could understand that. It wasn't a common occurrence that she met a girl who wanted to be a goalie and compete against guys.

"I just really love doing it," I said. "It comes naturally to me and I guess it's human nature to want to do things that we're good at. Don't you think?"

"I guess," she said, sounding somewhat unconvinced. "I hope you like the clothes I gave you. If you want, you can use our washer and dryer and wear your own stuff tomorrow. And Mom says she'll take us to the mall so you can buy some underwear, deodorant and any personal items you need."

"I can't thank you and your family enough for letting me stay here. I'm not sure what I would have done otherwise."

"My dad would have made sure you were billeted somewhere just like your brother and Iggy. Most of the players who are at the camp are billeted with members of the team."

The next morning, after a hearty breakfast cooked by Coach Sinclair himself, we headed back to the arena. I was really looking forward to seeing how I would do against Junior prospects. It was one thing to go against Juvenile players, but Junior hockey was a big leap up from there. The players were bigger and faster and had shots that could knock you over. I knew I had looked pretty good the day before, but who knew what these players had up their sleeve. If they were like my brothers, they would do almost anything to score on me.

Iggy was all suited up by the time we arrived. He was obviously keen to show his stuff. I was really hoping that he would do well so that maybe we both could play for the Hornets. Now wouldn't that be a coup?

I suited up and joined Iggy on the ice. The other players were doing warm ups and skating backwards. I always liked to start slow and work my way up to a good sweat. It didn't take long with all the equipment goalies had to wear. My skates were a bit of a problem as they weren't goalie skates and I missed my own. I would just have to do my best without them.

The practice went better than I expected. And Coach Sinclair couldn't say enough about my performance. He definitely treated me different from the way he treated the rest of the players. He was not complimentary toward them at all and released a whole lot of them on day two. Jed, thankfully, wasn't among them. And neither was Iggy.

I had never seen Iggy play so well. Obviously, he was taking these practices seriously and wanted to make the team as much as I wanted to. That surprised me as I often

thought Iggy wasn't terribly serious about being a goaltender. I always thought he looked at it as being something amusing, something to do until something real came
around. Maybe I had been wrong.

Almost half of the players packed up their gear and
headed home after that day's practice. I felt sorry for them.
It must have been hard. I know how I would have felt if
Coach Sinclair had told me to pack my gear and leave.
I would have been crushed. There weren't many things
that I had failed at and being the best goaltender I could
be was high on my priority list, even higher than getting
good grades and becoming a good pianist.

"You were terrific again, Katherine," Coach said in the
dressing room. "How do you feel you did today?"

"Great," I said. "These skates aren't the best, but I think
I'll survive."

"I'll see what I can do," he said. "There must be some
goalie skates around here somewhere that will fit you."

There was a whole crowd of us around the supper table
that night. Coach invited Jed and Iggy and then there were
his two daughters and his wife as well as himself. We were
quite a family. Coach was a real character and loved telling
stories about his daughters which made them blush and
shake their heads. I wasn't sure if what he was telling us
was the truth or an exaggeration but they were certainly
entertaining stories.

"Don't believe a word my Dad tells you," Silvia said
later in my room. "He loves to make us blush. I really
don't know where he gets all his ideas. He should have
been a writer he tells so many tall tales."

Silvia and I spent the evening listening to music and
talking about school. She wanted to come down to the

arena and see me in action the next day. She was very curious about my goalkeeping and what it was like. I also got the idea that she wouldn't mind seeing some of the boys in action.

The next day's practice was much different from the first two. Coach Sinclair had pared the hopefuls down to about 12 as well as Jed, Iggy and me. The other goalie had been sent packing so it looked like Iggy and I were going to be busy for the next few days.

Coach Sinclair concentrated on conditioning a lot and I think most of the players were beginning to wish they had never bothered attending the camp. It was hard on Iggy and me as well. Neither one of us was in great shape and Coach expected us to do pretty much what the other players had to do. By the end of the first half-hour, I was gasping for breath and so was Iggy. I guess the dry land training we did didn't transfer well to conditioning on the ice. Coach no doubt thought that if his prospects could withstand this much conditioning, they were the kind of players he wanted. I was relieved when we finally had some scrimmage and I had a chance to catch my breath.

Playing against potential Junior B players was quite challenging. They had a lot of moves that I hadn't seen before, but I was still able to stop most of what came my way. During a break, I skated over and talked to Silvia, who was sitting in the stands watching us being put through our paces.

"Wow! You must be exhausted," she said. "I don't know how you do it."

"Neither do I," I said. "I've never had to do this much skating in my life. And my feet are killing me. What I wouldn't do to have my own skates."

"You are really doing well," Silvia said. "Dad is really impressed. He thinks you might be his number one goalie this year. Wouldn't that be something? You would be making history around here. There's never been a girl that played hockey with the guys before."

"I haven't even thought that far ahead," I said. "I can't even get my head around making the team let alone moving away from my family for a year."

"You could live with us," Silvia said. "Wouldn't that be great? We could have so much fun together."

I could just imagine what my mother's reaction would be when that proposal came up. It was one thing playing in my own home town, but moving away at 16 and living with another family was something entirely different. My life was becoming very complicated.

The practice ended with more stops and starts and sprints as though we hadn't already had enough conditioning. I literally staggered into the dressing room.

Most of the young guys who were trying out were older than me by a year or two. I'm sure some of them didn't know what to make of me. Some of them were fairly friendly, but most did their best to ignore me. Of course, I had the same problem of getting dressed and undressed but there was a small room off the main one that I could use to change back into my street clothes. Once everybody had had their shower and was changed, I came back in for the talks that Coach Sinclair always had after the practices. He had a certain philosophy about playing hockey and he liked to impart that to his players so that they always knew where they stood and what they had to concentrate on to make the team. There were still about 12 players and of them only about 6 or 7 would be chosen.

Back at the house, Silvia, Sandra and their mom were going shopping and asked if I wanted to go with them. They didn't have to ask that twice. I didn't have any money to speak of, but I always enjoyed window shopping and looking at all the latest fashions. And it would give me a chance to look at Lakeland and see what kind of city it was. I had never been here before so everything was new to me.

We went to a huge mall where Silvia and I went off on our own for awhile and visited some of the shops, looked at lots of clothes and shoes, but of course we didn't buy anything. I think she was as broke as I was. Her mom treated us at the food court and by the time we arrived back, I felt as though I was one of the family. They were all so friendly that it was easy being with them.

I couldn't help wondering whether I would actually be moving here this fall. It all seemed so unreal. But if it did happen, it was comforting to think that Jed would be here too to look after me if anything happened. Maybe I was getting ahead of myself. Mom might really put her foot down and refuse to let me go and in a way, I wouldn't blame her. After all, I was only 16 and had never been on my own before.

The last day of the camp was a memorable one. It was the day the remaining hopeful would find out whether they were going to be playing for the Lakeland Hornets that year or not. Coach took it easy on us for a change. I guess he figured since it was the last day and he had already made his selections, that it didn't matter that much.

When the practice was over, Coach came into the dressing room and talked to the players and then told us who had made the team and who hadn't. Jed had made it of course. He was one of the best players and I knew the coach was pleased with him. But there were a lot of sad-looking hopefuls who hadn't been selected. The chosen ones made a lot of noise. Coach hadn't said anything to me or Iggy and I was kind of on pins and needles wondering what my fate might be. For some reason, he waited until the other players had left, before giving us the news.

"Katherine, we definitely want you to join our team this year. You've proven yourself to be an excellent goaltender, far beyond what I was expecting. It's just a matter of whether you want to be a part of our team or not. I know it means a big adjustment on your part, but we really want you to join us."

He turned to Iggy. "I'm sorry, Iggy, but I don't think you're quite ready. Perhaps next year. Unfortunately, I haven't got room for 3 goalies or else I would have you join us. But I was impressed with what you showed here. You've got great potential and I hope you'll return for a tryout next year."

There it was. I wasn't quite sure how I felt. I looked over at Iggy wondering how disappointed he was, but he was smiling like always.

"I knew you'd make it," he said. "Nice going. You were terrific as usual."

"Thanks Iggy," I said, not sure how I felt. It seemed a little empty since Iggy hadn't made the cut.

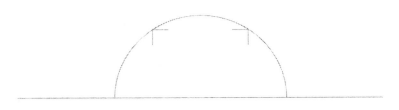

CHAPTER 11

When we got home that night, Mom was in the kitchen and Dad was in the living room reading the paper.

"Well how's my little Gump Worsely?" he asked, as I sat down beside him. "I hope you wowed them over there."

"I made the team," I said.

"Good for you," Dad said. "Helen, our little girl wowed them over at Lakeland. What do you think of our girl now?"

Mom appeared from the kitchen, came over and gave me a hug. "I'm glad you're home. I was a little worried about you."

"You didn't have to worry, Mom. I was fine. And Jed was there. He made the team too, but Iggy didn't."

"So what does that mean?" Mom wanted to know. "You made the team, but you live here. How are you going to play for them if you're 200 miles away?"

I was afraid Mom might ask me something like that. I wasn't quite sure how to answer her without getting her all upset.

"Well...ah...I might have to..."

"She might have to move there for the year," Jed said, "and so will I. There's no other solution."

Jed had always been one to come right out with the bald truth.

To say that Mom looked a little taken aback would be an exaggeration. She looked crushed. "Move there? How can you do that? You have to go to school. Your friends are here. We're here. You can't just up and leave."

I gave her my best "I don't know" look. Dad was suddenly finding his newspaper very interesting. Jed was smiling, obviously enjoying our family intrigue.

"Well, we can talk about it tomorrow," Mom said, as though I would have a change of mind overnight and everything would be back to normal.

"I would like to talk about it now," I heard myself say. "It's a big decision and I've made up my mind. I really want to play Junior hockey and if that means moving away for awhile, well, so be it. It's not as though I'm going to the other side of the earth. I'll be able to come home fairly often and you can come over and watch us play."

"Frank, talk to your daughter. I don't want her moving away like that. She's too young. It's just ridiculous."

Dad looked at me. "Do you really want to do this? Is it worth getting your mom all upset? Surely she has some say about it."

"I know." I tried to look unhappy about everything, but was having a hard time pulling it off. I was secretly overjoyed about the prospect of being the number one goalie for the Lakeland Hornets. Mom had no idea what a big deal this was. I was in the middle of making a little bit of hockey history. It was going to be a big story in the hockey world and I was reveling in it.

"Try to understand our position," Mom explained.
"You're our only daughter. You belong with your parents.
You belong in your own home...I'll miss you. And what
about your music?"

Mom was really pulling out all the stops and putting
the guilt trip on me. There had to be some way I could
convince her that the apron strings needed to be cut, if
only temporarily, and that I was still her little girl and
loved her just as much as I always had.

"I'll take piano lessons over there," I said. "There must
be lots of piano teachers in a city the size of Lakeland.
Of course, it won't be like taking them from you, but
it's better than nothing. And I'll miss you too, all of you,
but this is a once in a lifetime opportunity and I want to
take it."

There was a long pause during which nobody was
saying anything. I could almost feel Mom reloading. She
wasn't going to give in without a fight to the finish.

"Maybe we should take a vote," Jed offered. "There's
nothing like a little democracy in the family to keep
things humming along."

I looked hopefully over at Mom. I knew I would win if
it came to a vote. The twins would be overjoyed at getting
rid of me, Jed was on my side and I think Dad secretly
loved the idea of me playing Junior hockey. It would be
kind of a feather in his cap, something he could brag about
to his pals down at the mill.

"What do you think, Mom? Should we vote on it? I
promise to abide by whatever the vote turns out to be."
Now wasn't I being the brave one? It was a shoo in and I
knew it.

Mom shrugged and looked resigned. Maybe she knew what I knew – that if it came to a vote, she would probably be the only one who wanted me to stay.

Jed went to the stairs. "Hey you guys, we're having a family vote. Get down here."

After several minutes, the twins and Michael came thumping down the stairs. "Hey, look what the cat dragged in," John said, looking over at me.

"How was the tryout?" Michael wanted to know.

"It was fantastic," Jed said. "We both made the team. Katherine blew them away. Looks like she's going to be the Hornet's number one goalie."

"Really?" John said, looking dumbfounded. "Holy catfish."

"What's the vote about?" Malcolm asked.

"Mom doesn't want Kat moving to Lakeland and playing for the Hornets, so I suggested we have a vote," Jed said. "What do you guys say?"

"I think she should be able to go," Michael said. "It's a great opportunity."

"Yeah," Malcolm chimed in. "She should go." He looked over at his twin brother. "And I get her room."

"You can have it," John said. "I'll move into Jed's room."

"This isn't about who's going to get whose room," Jed said. "It's a vote. What do you say, John?"

"Let her go play for the Hornets. She'll get a real taste of how hard those guys can shoot. And I'll bet my allowance she won't get so many shutouts there."

"I vote that Katherine be allowed to go," Jed said. "That's three votes in favor. I know how you'll vote, Mom. How about you, Dad?"

Dad looked at Mom and then back at us. "I'm not so sure a decision like this should be decided by a family vote. It's too important for that. This should be a decision between your mother and me. As far as I'm concerned, I wouldn't like to stand in Katherine's way. I think it's a wonderful opportunity for her. But it's important to consider your mother's side of things."

Everybody looked at Mom. She didn't look happy, just sat there gazing into the distance. I wanted to go over and put my arms around her and assure her that everything would be all right, but before I could do anything, she stood up. "I don't want Katherine to go. She's too young. That's how I feel and I won't change my mind. But if she wants to go that badly, then I won't stop her." Without another word, she left the room, slamming the door behind her.

"It'll be all right," Dad said. "I'll talk to her. She'll come around."

I wasn't so sure about that. Sometimes Mom could be awful stubborn about things, especially things concerning her family.

The rest of the summer was a bit of a blur. I was anxious to make the move to Lakeland. Mom was acting as though I had committed the crime of the century and my brothers, well, they were their usual bothersome selves. Nothing ever seemed to change in that regard.

When September finally rolled around and I was going to have to leave, Mom got even more upset than she already was. I guess Dad had underestimated his ability to cajole his wife and assure her that I was sixteen, going on seventeen and had my own needs. I tried to talk to her a couple of times, but she wasn't prepared to listen at all. I had made up my mind and she didn't want me to leave and there didn't seem to be any middle ground.

I hated leaving with Mom still mad at me, but what could I do? When the day finally came and I had packed up all my stuff and loaded it in Jed's car, Mom wouldn't even come out and say goodbye and give me a hug. She stayed in her bedroom and wouldn't come out.

"I'm sorry about your mother," Dad said, giving me a hug. "Give 'em heck over there. Make us proud."

"I will," I said. "Say goodbye to Mom for me." I looked at the twins and Michael who were hovering around not sure how to react to our departure. I went over and gave each of them a hug. I think I shocked them more than I did myself. Puck was jumping around yelping and barking as though he knew that I wasn't soon coming back. I knelt down and gave him a big hug.

As we drove out of the yard, I looked up at Mom's bedroom window and could see her looking out. I wanted Jed to stop the car so I could run back and say a proper goodbye to Mom, but I knew it would be futile. Once Mom sets her mind to something, there was no changing it.

It took over 4 hours to reach Lakeland and Jed and I didn't have much to say to each other. I knew he was just as upset as I was about Mom, but talking about it would just make it all that much worse. I intended to write Mom a long letter once I got settled in and try to explain why I wanted to be a goaltender and why it was important to me to find my own way and do my own thing. Surely she would understand.

The whole Sinclair family was there to meet us when we arrived. They all seemed really excited about me staying with them. It was great to have such a warm reception and helped to dull my thoughts about leaving my own family, especially Mom.

They had fixed up a bedroom for me and in short order I had taken possession and felt about as much at home as it was possible to feel. Coach Sinclair insisted that I only pay board. As for the room, he said that it would sit empty anyway.

The next day I had to register at my new school. I was entering the eleventh grade, the same as Silvia.

"Maybe we'll be in the same class," she said. "I hope so."

I knew the hockey season didn't start for at least six weeks so I intended to use some of the time to first of all find a piano teacher and then do some practicing. It wasn't so much that I wanted to improve my piano playing, I was already as good as I wanted to be, but I knew Mom wanted me to keep up my lessons. If I couldn't please her by staying at home, the least I could do was ensure her that my music wasn't suffering.

I hadn't seen a piano in the Sinclair house, but when I asked about one, Coach Sinclair said that he knew where one was that he could borrow while I was living there. I could scarcely believe how kind and considerate a family they were. It seemed nothing was too difficult for them and they would literally go to the ends of the earth to make my stay enjoyable. I felt quite privileged.

I phoned home and talked to Dad and told him we had arrived safely and all. When I asked about Mom, he seemed a little evasive. "She's fine," he said. "How is your new place?"

I told him about my room and how thoughtful the whole family had been. He seemed pleased to hear from me. I asked to talk to Mom, but he said she was in the shower and that maybe I could talk to her next time I phoned. I was disappointed, but I doubted that Mom was ready to talk to me yet anyway.

The next day Jed came by and we went over to the Lakeland High School. Silvia came with us and showed us around the school. It was much bigger than our school in Smithville and had a lot more facilities. It was going to be strange attending a different school and making new friends.

I met a few of the teachers and discovered that the music teacher also taught piano so I was able to kill two birds with one stone so to speak and sign up for lessons.

Jed had a lot to do himself so he dropped us off at the mall and arranged to pick us up later. Silvia and I walked around the mall doing a lot of window shopping and dreaming. We ran into a few of her friends and together we had lunch at a small cafe nearby.

By the time Jed returned, we had trekked the length and breadth of the mall and were ready to go home. So much for my first day in Lakeland. The hockey season seemed a long way off. I would have preferred to hit the ice right away, but I knew I would have to be patient.

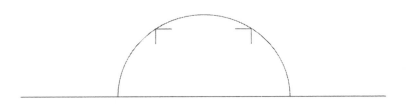

CHAPTER 12

During the six weeks prior to the hockey season, Silvia and I spent a lot of time together and the more I got to know her, the more I liked her. We had a lot in common and were becoming fast friends. I missed Tracy and talked to her on the phone a few times and Iggy drove over to see me one afternoon. It was great to see him again. He was planning to play Juvenile again for the Lumberjacks.

The first practice was really strange. It was wonderful to be skating again and I looked forward to the action. We didn't do much except skate on the first day. There were no pucks, just a lot of starts and stops and wind sprints. I was out of shape and was breathing really hard at the end.

Coach introduced me to the team. I'm not sure how I was perceived. Most of them looked at me as though I had two heads. They had never played with a female goaltender and I was a real novelty. The newest arrivals that had attended the tryout already knew me and most of them were quite friendly. The other goaltender ignored me completely. His name was Norman Swift, a perfect name for a goalie, I thought. I felt a little rejected as I had always had a good relationship with the other goalies on the teams I played on. Maybe he felt threatened. I hoped not. Coach had indicated that I was going to be his number one goalie. Perhaps Norman either didn't know that or considered himself to be number one. I hoped that would be cleared up as soon as possible. I hadn't seen him in action yet to be able to compare his prowess to mine.

Pucks appeared in our second practice and I was finally able to begin showing what I could do and perhaps discover whether or not I was ready for Junior hockey. I tried to keep an eye on Norman, but at first I was so busy in my own net, that it was difficult to see what he was like. It wasn't until I had a short break that I was finally able to size up my competition. To say that I was relieved is an understatement. Norman was competent, maybe even better than that, but I knew I was better than he was. Chalk one up for me.

I was pretty sure Norman was keeping an eye on me as well and when the practice was over, he finally skated up to me. "Hey, you're pretty good. Where'd you learn to play goal like that?"

I smiled up at him. I say "up" because he was about a foot taller than I am. "I just picked it up," I said. "Read some books and talked to a few old pros. How about you?"

He shrugged. "I've been playing in goal since I was about ten years old. I've been to a bunch of hockey schools. Played up through the ranks. I was the number one goalie here last year." The baleful look he gave me spoke volumes.

But you aren't going to be this year, I said to myself. Was he trying to send me a message?

In our first exhibition game against a Junior A team from Regina, Norman was in goal for the first period and a half. Regina had a lot of shots on goal and Norman was busier than he wanted to be. They scored three times in the first period, but things settled down in the second. By the time it was my turn to play, the score was 3 to 1.

There was a murmur throughout the crowd when I was announced and skated onto the ice. At last it was my turn to show what I could do.

I made several good saves before the end of the second period and kept the score at 3 to 1. Coach came and sat down beside me in the dressing room between periods. "You're doing great, Katherine. Just keep doing what you've been doing and we'll handle the rest."

As it turned out, we scored twice more, one of them by Jed, and the game ended 3 all. They hadn't scored on me and I was ecstatic. If a Junior A team couldn't beat me, I figured I was going to do all right playing Junior B.

A lot of people stayed around after the game to congratulate me on my stellar performance. I couldn't help noticing that a lot of them were women and girls. Was I setting an example for female athletes and sending a message that maybe women could compete with men in certain situations? I certainly hoped so. Being a role model for other girls was something that I would embrace with a great deal of enthusiasm.

Norman Swift didn't have a lot to say to me, but he did give me a nod which I interpreted as being a "nice game" comment. Jed, of course, was full of compliments. It was so great having an older brother on the same team.

Around the Sinclair table that night, the Coach and his wife Helen held up their glasses of wine and proposed a toast to me for my performance that afternoon. Of course we kids only had juice instead of wine, but the thought was just the same. Silvia was just as excited as I was and gave me a hug for about the tenth time. I felt really special. How was I ever going to repay this wonderful family for all that they had already done for me with the whole hockey season still ahead of us?

Our first league game was against the Brownsville Bruins, a team from a neighboring city about 50 miles away. There had been quite a rivalry between the two cities for several years and Coach was determined to start with a win. Norman got the call to start. To say that I was disappointed would be an understatement. But I knew I would just have to be patient and wait my turn. It would come, I was sure of that, but the sooner the better as far as I was concerned.

As it turned out, I didn't have to wait long. Before the half-way mark of the first period, the Bruins had scored 4 goals, a couple of which Norman should have been able to stop. Coach called a time out and signaled for me to take over in goal. As I passed Norman on the ice, he said, "Lots of luck" but it didn't sound as though he meant it. The crowd, which had up to this point been fairly quiet, suddenly started making a lot of noise. I tried my best to put everything out of my mind and concentrate one hundred percent on the job in front of me. After all, it was my debut into Junior hockey and I was determined to make a splash.

I shut down the Bruins for the rest of the game, and our guys began to get their game together. We scored the winning goal in the last minute and skated off with our first win.

Coach was excited to say the least. It was the first time in several years that the team had won their first game and he had a pat on the back for every player as they skated off the ice. Jed had scored another goal which made it even more special for me.

"That was just wonderful," Coach said to me, ruffling my hair and shaking his head as though he couldn't quite believe it all. "What do you think of this little gal, guys? Isn't she something else?"

There was a general agreement amongst the other players as they all banged their sticks on the floor. I looked over at Norman and he looked a little glum. I guess I couldn't blame him. Having his position taken away from him by a girl wasn't something many guys could get excited about. Somehow I was going to have to make a friend of him and try to avert any bad feelings that might occur in the future.

At school the next day, a lot of the students suddenly recognized me and offered their congratulations. Being new at a very large high school was a challenge, but now that I was becoming better known, it made things much easier. I didn't feel quite so isolated as I had felt for the first few weeks of the school year. It was great having Silvia as a friend, as she knew a lot of girls and introduced me around during the first few days of the semester.

I missed my friends from my old school, especially Tracy, but tried my best to keep up a correspondence with her through the telephone and the odd letter. It was great finding out about what everybody was doing. Dad mentioned that he would try to get over for one of my games as soon as he could and bring my brothers with him. He didn't mention Mom so I guess she still hadn't accepted the fact that I was going to be spending most of the year away from home.

I was enjoying my experience with the Hornets and felt that I was getting better after each practice. The players were becoming much friendlier and accepting me more as time went on. I guess since I might be the reason they won a lot of their games, that they should give me the credit that I deserved.

There were six teams in our league and Lakeland had never done particularly well in years past. They had most often been about in the middle of the pack, losing almost as many games as they had won. I hoped to be able to change that. Since I was the last bastion of hope after the defense, it was up to me to keep the games close and give our guys a good chance of winning.

Traveling from one city to the next posed a bit of a problem. We traveled by bus and most of the time I sat with Jed, but Jed was making friends of his own and didn't always want me hanging around him. I could understand that. Who would want their little sister as their constant companion even though our relationship was really good? I often just sat by myself or with Coach to give Jed a chance to make friends with the other team members. It also afforded me the opportunity to become more independent. I would have dearly loved to have another female on the team. The guys curtailed their swearing and off-color jokes since there was a girl in their midst. I'm sure they didn't appreciate not being able to talk the way they were used to, but maybe that was a good thing. Making friends with the guys wasn't that easy and if I started hanging out with some of them, there was danger in that too, not that any of them had tried to become my buddy.

Most of them were friendly but standoffish. However, they weren't standoffish with each other and often a lot of kidding and skirmishes occurred that was reminiscent of how my brothers behaved with each other.

Our second game was against one of the weaker teams in the league about 80 miles from Lakeland. They were called the Sheffield Golden Hawks. Coach put Norman in goal which didn't bother me at all as Norman needed a game under his belt and especially a win to give him confidence. He didn't play too badly and I complimented him on his performance after the game. Norman was all smiles even though he let in a couple of easy goals. But our team outscored them and we won 6 to 2. Since Sheffield was so close to Lakeland, we didn't stay over but returned home that night on the bus. Whenever we had to stay over, we stayed in a motel. The team raised a lot of money by raffling off a house each year and combined with ticket sales for the home games, a fair amount of money was raised. Transportation costs and accommodation were very expensive and the team needed every cent they could raise to pay for these costs.

The year I spent in Lakeland seemed long and a little dragged out. I missed being at home constantly and I missed the companionship of my mom. Even though playing in goal was exciting and I seemed to be making a name for myself, it didn't compare to being with my family and friends. Had I made a mistake by leaving and in the process hurting my mom so badly that she wouldn't even talk to me on the phone? She was always busy doing something when I called. I had written her several letters, but she hadn't answered them. I knew Mom was stubborn but she was carrying this a little too far.

People here stopped me on the street and complimented me on my performances. I had several shutouts which I was most proud of and it was rare for the other team to score more than 2 goals on me. Coach told me that the crowds were almost double from last year and he attributed it to me. I was a peculiarity, a rarity that attracted a lot of attention. People really wanted to see a girl playing against guys and succeeding. There weren't many sports where that could happen.

Dad and my brothers came to a home game and it was one of my best outings. In fact, I almost got a shutout. I got scored on in the last minute, but it was a meaningless goal and we won easily. It was great seeing Dad and even the twins were semi-civilized. Dad took us all out to a restaurant after the game and we all talked up a storm. It was almost as good as being at home except that Mom wasn't there. Later we went over to the Sinclair's house and Dad met the whole family. He seemed to like them as much as I did.

When Christmas came and Jed and I went home, Mom seemed distracted. She didn't want to discuss what I was doing, how I felt, what I had accomplished. Even when I told her about my new music teacher and how I was progressing, she only seemed mildly interested.

"That's nice, dear," was about all I could get out of her.

"She really misses you," Dad said. "But she'll never admit it. You'll just have to give her time."

When it was time to return to Lakeland after Christmas, Mom was nowhere to be found. Didn't she want to see me off, wish me luck, give me a hug, tell me she cared about me? After all, I was her only daughter and we had always been very close. I hated pulling away from the house without saying goodbye. Why was Mom doing this? Was she punishing me for leaving? After all, we had had a vote hadn't we and the majority agreed that I should spend the year in Lakeland. If I had known then how this was going to affect her, I don't think I would have gone.

"You're taking this altogether too seriously, Kat," Jed said on the trip back to Lakeland. "Mom is acting like a child. That's not your fault. It's hers. She needs to smarten up and start acting like a parent, not like some spoiled teenager who didn't get her own way."

"But I've never known her to be like this," I said. "It's so unlike her."

"Maybe she's got other things on her mind or maybe she's entering menopause. Who knows?"

"Jed, she's too young to be in menopause for heaven's sake. She's only in her early forties."

"Stranger things have happened," Jed said.

My year in Lakeland, although a lonely one without my family, was marked by a number of accomplishments. I had several shutouts and was voted Most Valuable Player at the end of the year. I made strides in my music mainly because of my new music teacher who was wonderfully encouraging. The Sinclair family were simply marvelous and couldn't do enough for me. I became almost like one of the family and was treated as such. I had made a lifelong friend of Silvia as well as her family and would continue to visit them in the future.

It was especially helpful having the coach nearby as he enjoyed talking hockey and this gave me a lot of insights into how to play smarter, how to get along well with the other players and he always complimented me and made me feel good about my game. If he had a criticism, it was always constructive and he always began it with a compliment that made it easier to accept.

I was eager to get home at the end of the year, but had to finish out my grade 11 at Lakeland High. It would have been much too disruptive to transfer back in March even though I would have preferred that. When we finally did go home, I was apprehensive about how Mom was going to react to my returning. Would she be like her old self or would she still treat me as though I was a leper?

As it turned out, Mom's recital was on the same day I was coming home. I had an idea that might help to break the ice between us and phoned Iggy to tell him about it and to get him to help me. I wanted to surprise Mom with how well I was playing the piano. I thought it would be interesting if I was able to sneak in a solo at the end of the recital before she realized what was going on. I told Iggy all about it and he thought it was a good idea. What I needed from Iggy was for him to distract my mom for a few minutes, while I set myself up at the piano and began my piece. Could it be done? Iggy thought so and agreed to co-operate.

I was as nervous as a cat at a dog show as we approached the church where the recital was to be held. Iggy had assured me that Mom didn't have a clue I was coming or that I would be playing a piece at the end of the recital. Jed and I sneaked into the back of the church and hid ourselves the best we could. When the last performance was in progress, we had to wait uncomfortably for several minutes for it to end. Finally, after the applause, and Mom had disappeared backstage, I rushed down the aisle saying hello to many of the parents that I knew and went over and sat at the piano.

"If you could wait just a few minutes," I announced. "I would like to play a piece for you that I have been practicing for awhile."

Everybody sat down again and I began my recital. I had chosen a piece by Rachmaninoff, a concerto that I knew was one of Mom's favorites. Although I was nervous and a little out of breath, I began playing. Before long, I got right into the spirit of the piece and finally ended with a flourish. There was a momentary silence when I finished and then all the parents stood up and applauded and yelled "Bravo". It was a moment that I will savor for a long time, hardly daring to look to see if Mom had heard me play. And then I saw her rushing toward me.

"Oh Kat darling, that was beautiful," she said as I stood up and we embraced. "What a lovely surprise. And what a perfect piece to play. Oh darling, I'm so glad you're home. I've missed you so much."

Jed approached and Mom gave him a hug too. She seemed like her old self again and I felt a relief that I hadn't felt for the whole year. My mom was back and everything would be like it had been before. What more could I have hoped for?

After talking to several of the people at the recital, Jed and I drove home closely followed by Mom. "Guess your little scheme worked out pretty well," Jed said. "Congratulations."

I grinned over at him. "It's nice to see her back to her old self again, don't you think?"

"You can say that again."

It was wonderful to be home again, but especially so because Mom was back to normal. My brothers were even glad to see me.

"Are you going back next year?" Michael wanted to know.

I looked over at Mom. She was regarding me with an anxious look on her face.

"Coach wants me to, but I don't think I will. I want to graduate with my friends. And I missed you guys, especially you Mom. It'll be my last year at home anyway so I want to make the most of it."

Mom came and put her arms around me. "I'm so glad to hear that, dear. I was afraid you were going to leave us again for another year and I don't think I could bear it. We all want you home where you belong."

"I think you're crazy," Malcolm said. "If I had the opportunity to play Junior hockey, I'd jump at it."

"Now you just mind your P's and Q's," Mom said. "If Katherine has made up her mind to stay home, I don't want you trying to influence her."

"No fear of that," I said. "I've given it a lot of thought and I've made up my mind."

"Are you going to play Juvenile again?" John asked. "Quite a comedown if you ask me."

"I might, especially if you guys are playing on my team. That might be kind of fun."

The twins looked at each other not sure how to respond to that statement.

"We could call ourselves the Rollins Four if we all ended up on the same team," Michael said. "We'd be a force to be reckoned with."

That night around the supper table, my dad offered a toast. "To Katherine and Jed," he said. "Welcome back to the family. We've missed you more than we can say."

Glenn **PARKER**

For the first time in weeks, I felt at peace. There was nothing like being at home again even though the Sinclairs had made me feel like a part of their family.

I looked forward to the coming year with the hope that it would be successful and that our family harmony would be as wonderful as it was today.

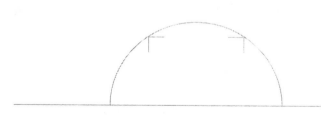

EPILOGUE

(June, 1990)

Iggy and I were married today on our front lawn, just beside our skating rink which isn't a skating rink right now, but just bare ground waiting for the cold weather. Tracy is here as well as Silvia and her whole family. I couldn't believe that they would make the long trip from Lakeland, but they said they wouldn't have missed it for anything.

A lot has happened in the last 6 years. I won an athletic scholarship to the University of Colorado and played in goal for the women's team for four years. I was nominated Most Valuable Player every year that I played and had more shutouts than any previous goaltender in their history. I was invited to try out for the Canadian National Team but declined. After four years of stopping pucks and traveling I don't know how many miles, I felt it was time for me to hang up my goalie pads.

I managed to get my degree in Social Work and have been employed by the Health Department in Smithville ever since. I'm also teaching piano to half-a-dozen students. Iggy became a lawyer and has recently opened an office in town. We are in the process of buying a house no more than a few miles from here. After being at university for four years, coming home and settling here has been a dream come true. As you can imagine, my mom was thrilled not only that I wanted to return and settle nearby, but that I am marrying a young man she and my dad approve of most highly.

Jed graduated to a Junior A team and played a year with them. He now lives here in Smithville with his girlfriend and works at the mill with my dad. The twins and Michael are at university. Malcolm is working on a master's degree in Phys Ed and John wants to be a math teacher. Michael is in his last year of chartered accountancy. They are all here, however, to attend our wedding.

I look back at my goal tending career with a lot of pride. That I had taken up a preoccupation that belongs almost exclusively to the male gender, was quite amazing. Competing all those years with young men gave me a lot of satisfaction and self-confidence. I'm somewhat amazed that I never got seriously injured and that I was accepted so readily wherever I played. It has been a wild ride that I wouldn't have missed for anything.

And when I reflect on all those cold mornings when my brothers and I played on our home made hockey rink, I have to smile. What in the world ever made me want to get up out of a warm bed, put on a whole lot of heavy equipment and then let my brothers fire a rubber disc at me? When I think about it, it seems rather curious. But it started me on the road to an interesting and challenging endeavor that involved my whole family. And we all became the better for it. Even my twin brothers who could never score on me but never complained....not!

I hope that I have blazed a trail for other young girls to follow. I've learned how important it is to follow your dreams, and not to be discouraged just because nobody else has done what you hope to do, and to keep on going forward despite the negativity and naysayers. After all, it is your life and fulfilling your dreams is about as important as it gets. Regret is the alternative and nobody wants to live with that.

Just as an interesting aside, my family made history in my last year of school, when three of my brothers and I played on the same team and set an undefeated record that might never be broken. It was definitely a year to remember. However, the most interesting part of that family affair was that dad came out and coached our team, a fact that still astounds me today. It was a brave thing for him to do. Was he a good coach? I think our undefeated record answers that question. Nice going, Dad, and thank you.

Note: Katherine Rollins was responsible for giving female goalkeepers the voice and recognition they deserved by forming MAGGI (Masked Association of Girl Goalies International) that brought them together as a group to discuss their particular problems and encourage young women to become goalies and offer them support. The group was formed in 1985 and has since grown to over 150 members which includes alumni as well as current players. Katherine served as its president for several years while playing for the University of Colorado.

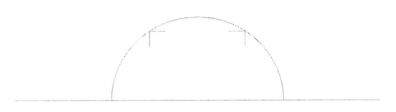

ABOUT THE
Author

This is Glenn Parker's first novel. He has written and published numerous short stories both in the U.S. and New Zealand. Mr. Parker taught English for 25 years in British Columbia and New Zealand. He played midget, juvenile, intermediate and university hockey for the University of British Columbia Thunderbirds under Father Bauer. He and his wife live in Comox, British Columbia and travel extensively. His interests include reading, doing crosswords and playing as much golf as the weather allows.

CPSIA information can be obtained at www.ICGtesting.com
Printed in the USA
LVOW10s1121071014

407645LV00001B/18/P